ROGUE AGENT

"Guess who Wilson really was?"

"Amelia Earhart?"

"He was exactly who he said he was. Everything checks out. He was one of us, Sam. Paine killed a serving member of the Central Intelligence Agency."

"Christ, what the hell do you think happened over there?"

"It's obvious. Paine's gone over. Wilson found out about it and tried to stop him. End of Wilson. Paine gets out— mighty easily—and back into the waiting arms of the CIA. It's obvious, Sam. Paine's a double."

"No he isn't."

Sullivan sat down and smiled. "Why don't we run it by Langley and see what they say?"

JACK DRAKE

AVON BOOKS ◆ NEW YORK

ROGUE AGENT is an original publication of Avon Books. This work has never before appeared in book form. This work is a novel. Any similarity to actual persons or events is purely coincidental.

AVON BOOKS
A division of
The Hearst Corporation
105 Madison Avenue
New York, New York 10016

Copyright © 1991 by Robert Tine
Hard to Kill excerpt copyright © 1991 by Robert Tine
Published by arrangement with the author
Library of Congress Catalog Card Number: 89-91926
ISBN: 0-380-75988-8

First Avon Books Printing: February 1991

AVON TRADEMARK REG. U.S. PAT. OFF. AND IN OTHER COUNTRIES, MARCA REGISTRADA, HECHO EN U.S.A.

Printed in the U.S.A.

RA 10 9 8 7 6 5 4 3 2 1

1

The American was drunk, as usual.

He had come stumbling down the steps of the club at 1:30 A.M., right on time, not noticing the smirk of the concierge or the quick, knowing glances exchanged by the bar girls. Enzo, the bartender, had put a coaster and a drink down on the counter before the American had settled on his stool.

The American was everyone's favorite customer at the Club Paradiso: He was stupid and rich. He never noticed that his "Courvoisier" was about as French as a french fry (it was, in fact, a villainous brew concocted by the bartender's brother-in-law on the outskirts of Rome); he never noticed how outrageously his bill was padded with charges for "champagne" his female companions—employees of the club—had not drunk; he never noticed that the midnight snack the girls cajoled him into buying cost as much as a four-course dinner in a fine restaurant; he paid no mind to the huge service charge tacked onto his bill at the end of the evening. He just paid, grinning like a jackass and thought that the girls and the bartender liked him for himself.

"Evening, Signor Winston," said Enzo.

"Hiya, Enzo." Jerry Winston smiled the crooked smile of a drunk. "How's it hanging?"

Enzo showed his teeth in what passed for a smile. "I am fine." Enzo did not speak English quite as well as he, or Winston, thought. "The weather is fine."

"Fuckin' fine," said Winston. "Weather's always fine in sunny Italy."

"Yessir."

"How's them bambinos of yours?"

"Fine, sir."

"Good." Winston slurped down some brandy, a gulp so big that Enzo—who knew well how terrible his brother-in-law's liquor was—almost winced watching. The American would poison himself one day if he continued to ingest such quantities of the evil brew.

"Lemme give you a piece of advice, Enzo." Winston slapped the bar emphatically. "Never, *never*, get involved in a dinner with soil erosion experts working in the Sudan. Bore your balls blue."

"Sir?"

"Bore your balls blue." Winston spoke loud enough for the other patrons of the bar to look in his direction. They scowled. Noisy drunks weren't welcome in the Club Paradiso—unless they had more money than everybody else. Men who came to the Paradiso came to meet women of a certain profession, men who had snuck away from their wives or who had left them at home while they enjoyed a Roman holiday. No one wanted any attention drawn to the place or their illicit activities.

There were a number of places like the Club Paradiso in Rome, most of them just off the Via Veneto, a street that had once enjoyed a certain notoriety, about thirty years before, as the home of *La Dolce Vita*—the late fifties sweet life, when the street was a magnet for stars, starlets, millionaires, and beautiful women. Today it was a street ruined by tourists who sat at the outdoor cafés gawking at each other, hoping to see Sophia Loren. They didn't know she lived in Switzerland. The Club Paradiso and clubs like it traded a little on the old glory of the neighborhood and lured horny, drunk out-of-towners off the streets with promises of beautiful women who would go home with you at the evening's end.

The Paradiso claimed to be an establishment of high style, with pretensions to exclusivity—completely false, of course—so the lights were kept low, so dim, in fact, that the patrons could not make out the careworn look of the place, the threadbare carpet and the upholstered sofas pockmarked with cigarette burns. The lighting flattered the girls too.

Winston put a cigar in his mouth, and Enzo, ever attentive, lit it for him.

"Much obliged. Had dinner at a place called Orso. Know it?"

"Osteria dell'Orso, yes," said Enzo. It was perhaps the most expensive restaurant in Rome. This American had probably spent three hundred dollars on dinner, and he would be fleeced of another two hundred fifty in the Paradiso; Enzo was impressed. The Americans claimed they were poor now, that it was the Japanese who had the money these days, but Mr. Jerry Winston never seemed to be short of cash.

"Hi, Jerry," said one of the girls, leaning over to kiss the American's cheek.

"Hi, hon," said Jerry. He pinched her breast and she jumped back, cradling her breasts in her arm. "Jerry!" she squeaked.

Winston slid an arm around her waist. "Enzo, give . . . give her a drink."

The woman pouted, forming her red lips into a little moue. "You don't remember my name, Jerry . . ."

Winston stared at her for a moment, closing one eye to focus on her heavily made-up face. "Sure I do. You're . . . you're Sonia."

"I am Anna."

Jerry slapped the bar and brayed with laughter. "Anna! That's right. That was my next guess. Siddown, Anna, and have a drink with me." Anna slid onto the stool next to him and squeezed his thigh as she did so.

Enzo slid the champagne bottle out of the speed rack and poured a glassful of sparkling grape juice.

"I was just saying to Enzo here that you should never get involved with guys in soil erosion. They are the most boring guys in the world. I used to think that it was the water guys who were the worst, always talking about artesian wells and iodine levels, but tonight I decided that it was the soil guys who are the worst. The absolute worst."

"Yes?" said Anna.

"I mean, it's not like what I do is fascinating— finance—but at least money is interesting."

"Yes," said Anna decisively. Money was a subject of much interest to her.

Enzo rolled his eyes. As best he could understand, Winston had something to do with the UN agency, the Food and Agriculture Organization, a giant agency based in Rome and dedicated to improving agriculture in the Third World. Winston was actually based in New York, at the UN headquarters, but he had been sent to Rome for a couple of months on special assignment.

Anna grazed his cheek with her lips. "I'm hungry."

"Enzo. The lady is hungry."

Anna rolled her eyes and smirked. Enzo called the kitchen and ordered some sandwiches, which arrived a few minutes later. They had been made the day before, thin slices of white bread and some fishy paste in the middle that the Club Paradiso called caviar.

Anna had a couple of drinks, nibbled one of the sandwiches, and then fled. Her place was taken by another girl, who was genuinely happy to sit with Jerry, not because she liked him, but to escape another client, a taciturn young man who had only bought her two drinks and didn't have much to say.

The young man watched his escort leave him and was glad to be alone. He sat in the gloom and watched the American slugging back his drinks, mauling the girls, and laughing like a mule. The young man was dark-complected and stylishly—or so he thought—dressed in a silk shirt open to the waist, showing a profusion of gold chains glistening on a hairy chest, tight white pants, and zip-up short boots with stacked heels. He looked with distaste at Jerry's baggy Brooks Brothers suit, blue shirt, and rep tie. Americans had no style, he thought.

The Italian *carta d'identità* in the young man's little shoulder bag identified him as Miguel Antonios of the Island of Malta, living in Italy on a student visa. The document was real, not forged, and no Italian policeman would have cause to detain him—unless he found the small-caliber pistol nestled in the bag next to his pack of Marlboros and his slim little mother-of-pearl cigarette lighter.

Miguel Antonios's real name was Ali Akbar Mahoud, and he had been born in the Sabra refugee camp in Lebanon; he was a member of the Popular Front for the Liberation of Palestine—or at least he would be, when he used his revolver to kill Jerry Winston later that night. Until the death of the American was fact, he was nothing more than a novice, unblooded in the fight for... Ali didn't really know what it was he was fighting. All he knew was that he had been instructed to hate Americans, and so he did. The PFLP had pulled him out of the camps, had dressed him well, and had given him money. For that he had been grateful, and he was prepared to kill to show his thanks and in the hope that the organization would give him more money, clothes, perhaps a car and a new base in Paris or London, where the girls were blond and, he had heard, whores.

Ali watched as Jerry Winston stood up and unsteadily made his way across the worn shag toward the bathroom. He passed Ali without a glance. The young man sipped his drink, then rose and followed.

Winston was standing at the urinal, his forehead resting on the water tank above the trough; he was fumbling in his pants and mumbling to himself. Ali took his place at a urinal a few places away and waited.

"You know what, pal?" said Winston.

Ali looked up. "Yes?"

"You know the trouble with this place? This fuckin' Club Paradiso?"

"Yes?" Ali spoke English, but not terribly well.

"The girls. They don't fuck, you know what I'm saying? They promise you everything, but they don't deliver shit."

"Yes?"

"You have that problem?"

"Yes."

"I mean, this is a shit town, for that kind of thing. You seen them hookers out on the Via Veneto? Look like my gran'mother. You know?"

"Yes."

"I mean, it's not like Manila or Thailand. Man, in Bangkok you can really have some fun. You like fun?"

"Yes."

"Where the hell do you find it in this town? Fuckin' dead. 'Cause of the Pope. You know the Pope lives here."

"Yes."

"You got a town with a Pope in it and you know it's going to be one stiff town, you know."

"Yes."

Winston was zipping up his pants. He ran his hands under cold water, looked at himself in the mirror, stuck out his tongue, and straightened his tie.

"Well, so long," he said. "Nice talking to you."

Ali forced himself to speak. "I know a place

... I know a place where the girls are very beautiful and they like to fuck."

Winston swayed toward the door. "Suuuure ... I heard that before."

"No, it's true. It is a *casa chiusa*. A whorehouse. Very high-class, very chic. Very beautiful girls. Not like this place; this place is for shit."

"Damn straight," said Winston emphatically.

"I take you there," said Ali.

Winston leaned against the tile walls and pulled a cigar out of his pocket. "Oh, I get it. You're a pimp. You know, I kinda thought you looked like a pimp. You know, the way you dress and all, you do sorta remind me of some fuckin' greasy little pimp. But, you know, no offense ..."

Ali colored deeply. He was sure if he had his shoulder bag with him, he would have pulled out his gun and shot the American then and there.

"Or maybe a faggot. You know, with them tight pants and those fuckin' shoes. A guy follows you into a washroom and he's dressed like that, what are you going to think: pimp or faggot or maybe both, right?"

"Shuttup!"

Winston looked genuinely surprised; he raised his hands and backed off. "Hey, sorry, pal. I didn't mean anything. I was just making conversation, you know, just chewing the fat. I

9

thought you Eyetalians had a good sense of humor."

Ali struggled to control himself. He wanted to hit the American, but drunk or not, Winston was a big man, broad in the shoulders and tall. Sober, he could probably kill Ali; drunk, he could do some damage. Better to make friends again and follow the plan; that was one thing he had been taught—always follow the plan.

Ali forced himself to smile. "I not speak English good. Now I see you were making a joke."

"Yeah, that's right. A joke. So where do we find this pussy you were talking about?"

"You come with me."

"Now?"

Ali glanced at his watch. Normally he took a long time looking at his watch, a gold Tissot, gleaming with dials and buttons, and waterproof to eight atmospheres. The happiest moments of Ali's life were when someone asked him the time. His watch was the first thing he had bought with his first payment. In the camp he had dreamed of having a watch like that. Winston's watch, he noticed, was a poor thing, as slim as a wafer, with only one dial showing—how boring—the time, and Xs and Vs where the numbers were supposed to be.

It was too early; the plan had been for later. But if he let Winston go back to his drink, he might get too drunk or more interested in one of the Paradiso girls. Ali had to act now.

"We go. I show you where."

"Gotta pay the bill," said Winston.

Enzo presented the check with a flourish. It was for three hundred thousand lire, about $270. Winston produced a roll of bills, stripped off three hundred-thousand lire notes, and slapped them on the bar. Enzo smiled; it was tip time. The service charge on the bill went to the club. Any money Enzo made came from the customers, and Winston usually gave him fifty thousand lire; he had come to expect it. Winston pulled out a pink fifty-thousand note, held it in the air over the bar for a moment. Enzo looked at the bill the way a dog stares at a treat; then Winston stuffed the note back into his pants.

"Nawww, not tonight, Enzo. You gonna start to take me for granted." Winston tapped Ali on the shoulder. "Lead on, McDuff," he said.

Enzo watched them go. *"Porca miseria,"* he cursed under his breath.

Winston followed his newfound friend up the Via Veneto. The sidewalks were deserted at that time of night, except for the off-duty cab drivers who came to the twenty-four-hour newsstand to get the early editions of the next day's paper, and the touts who tried to lure the stray tourist into clip joints like the Paradiso.

"Nightclub," one of them stage-whispered as they passed. "You want nightclub? Nice girl? Good drink? Floor show?"

Winston slowed down. "Girls?"

The tout smiled, anxious, eager to please. "Very nice. Very pretty."

11

"Hey," said Winston, calling to Ali. "This guy says he's got a good place."

The young man pulled him away. "I know a better place."

The tout, who was paid by the number of hapless drunks he pulled into his club, refused to give up. He followed them up the street. "Nice girl, good drink, floor show," he said over and over again like an incantation. "Come with me please."

Ali turned on him and let loose with a stream of Italian invective. The nightclub tout looked unhappy. "Nice girl?" he tried one more time.

"Sorry, pal," said Winston, "gotta go with my friend."

They crossed the street, walked under the arch in the old Roman wall, and crossed the Corso d'Italia; the young man strode purposefully ahead, leading the way into the dark of the Borghese Gardens, the largest park in the center of Rome. Winston stumbled after him, then stopped in the deep gloom as if suddenly aware of where he was.

"Hey, where the fuck we going anyway? This is a park, for God's sake. You didn't say we were going to a park."

"The place is on the other side of the park. This is a shortcut."

"The hell with that; let's get a cab." Winston started back toward the bright lights of the Via Veneto.

Ali panicked. "No, no, this way. Don't go back

there." He tried to drag Winston farther into the darkness, but the American threw him off.

"Hey! What the hell do you think? You think I was born yesterday? You're trying to get me to go into a park in the middle of the goddamn night? What kind of bullshit is that? I think you're a mugger or a fag. Either way, I'm not interested."

Ali was sweating so heavily, his silk shirt was soaked. "No, please, really. This is the way to a nice *casa chiusa*, with the girls. It is on the other side of the park. Five minutes and we are there."

Winston looked at him cannily. "How do I know I can trust you? A lot of strange things happen in parks after dark, you know. I think this is a setup."

"Please, you must trust me." The young man looked pleadingly at the big American. There must have been something in the look that reassured Winston, because he smiled.

"Okay, okay. I'll come with you, but just so I know I can trust you, I want you to do something for me . . ."

"Yes please, what?"

"Gimme your watch."

The young man stared at him, uncomprehending. "What?"

"I said you give me your watch. To hold, you know, like a security deposit. You let me hold your watch until we're at the whorehouse and then I'll give it back. If I've got your watch, then you'll behave yourself, right?"

"I cannot."

Winston shrugged and turned on his heel. "S'long, pal." He started back up the path that lead to the Via Veneto and the welcoming bright lights of the city. Ali gulped and wiped the sweat from his forehead. Everything was going wrong. His instructions were to lure the American into the park, by the big statue, where another member of the PFLP would meet him to provide backup. If Ali failed to perform, then he would be disgraced, possibly even expelled from the movement. There was even a chance that the punishment would be more harsh. There was only one thing to do. He unbuckled his watch.

"Wait! Wait!"

Winston, ten yards away now, stopped and turned. He saw Ali holding out the watch as if it were a peace offering.

"You can trust me."

Winston grinned, walked back, and took the watch. "C'mon, pal," he said, "let's go get laid."

The walked together into the darkness, the park silent around them. The sky was dully lit with the glare of the suburb of Parioli off to their right, but within the park itself, all was darkness, except the feeble light of a half moon.

"Peaceful," said Winston.

"Yes," said Ali Akbar.

"You know, this is a fine watch." Winston held

the timepiece close to his eyes, peering at it in the gloom. "Really nice."

"It is a Tissot," said Ali proudly.

"Tissot," Winston repeated, as if measuring the word. Then he smiled broadly. "Hey, pal, you know what Tissot is backwards?"

Ali was a few yards ahead of him. He stopped and turned. "What?"

"Backwards."

"Backwards?"

"Tissot backwards is 'toss-it,'" said Winston with a grin. "Here, catch." He fired the watch at Ali as if he were throwing a major league fastball. The watch zipped by Ali's outstretched hands and slapped against the base of a statue at the side of the footpath. There was the tinkling sound of breaking glass.

Ali shrieked and fell on his knees, as if in worship, at the base of the statue. He scrabbled in the gravel and finally found his mangled watch. He held it tight as if his touch could restore it to life. Winston, calmly, lit one of his cigars.

"Sorry about that, pal." He blew out the match and tossed it away. "It's only a fuckin' watch."

Ali jumped up and threw himself on Winston, screaming obscenities and kicking out blindly. Jerry Winston toppled to the ground. He smacked his head on the base of the statue, and Ali screamed with pleasure, hoping that the American had hurt himself badly.

"Hey, what the hell is going on, pal?" said Winston groggily. "What the hell you all hot about? I'll pay for the piece-of-shit watch; Christ, it's only worth about a couple of hundred bucks."

Ali's eyes blazed. "I kill you."

"You don't have to do that..." Winston staggered to his feet and stumbled toward Ali. The young man tore open his shoulder bag and pulled out his little gun.

"Stop!"

"C'mon, I was just foolin'—" Winston struck a match. In the flare of the flame, he saw the gun and stopped. "Is that a gun?"

"Yes. Now you die."

"Over a watch?" yelled Winston in disbelief.

"Kneel down at my feet," ordered Ali. Somewhere in his brain he was happy that the American had ruined his beautiful watch. Up until then he had doubted his ability to kill. Now he was sure he could do it, and what's more, enjoy it.

"Look, kid, I'll buy you a new watch. I'll buy you ten fuckin' Rolexes, whatever the hell you want."

"Be quiet! Get down on your knees!"

Winston sank to the ground.

Ali pressed his small gun to the base of the American's skull. "Are you scared, pig?"

"Yeah," said Winston soberly, "I'm scared."

"Good!"

There was the sound of footsteps on the gravel

2
___

The American Embassy in Rome is an imposing palace on the Via Veneto, once the summer home of the Queen of Italy. It is set in the midst of manicured lawns, beautifully tended gardens, and a tight ring of security. Two sets of Italian paramilitary police guard the gate, and the grounds are patrolled constantly by heavily armed agents. A spit-and-polish Marine sergeant sits behind four inches of bullet-proof glass in the reception area armed with a giant Smith & Wesson revolver and a pump-action Winchester at the ready. Getting in is not easy: Americans coming to report a stolen passport are treated as if they are terrorists, and Italians who have official business at the Embassy receive all the care, attention, and goodwill accorded an unexploded bomb. It is not a friendly place.

John Paine and Walter Hapgood bypassed the strict security, although the Marine on duty that night looked askance at Paine's disheveled clothing and his skinned knuckles. Still, the sergeant on duty knew better than to show his disapproval. Hapgood, one of the resident spooks, got a crisp salute, and Paine, something of an unknown quantity, a short nod. They were buzzed through the security doors, and before they got to the elevator, the Marine had advised the floor guards that two men were going up to the third floor, home of the cultural section, which also housed the offices of Central Intelligence.

The night duty officer in the intelligence office looked up from his desk as the two men arrived and buzzed them through the last set of security doors.

"You can go right in; he's waiting."

Walter Hapgood swept open the wide mahogany doors and ushered Paine into the office ahead of him, as if he were a headwaiter. The office was luxuriously furnished with a thick carpet on the floor overlaid with richly colored Persian rugs. The walls were paneled in dark cherry wood, and the ceiling extravagantly frescoed with voluptuous maidens representing the Graces. At the far end of the room was a huge desk, bare except for two telephones and a pen set. Behind the desk, sitting in a tall-backed green leather chair, was a pink-faced young man wearing a tweed suit and a floppy bow tie, Hapgood's immediate superior, Paul Cannon.

He glanced up from a file he was reading,

motioned toward two chairs that stood before his desk, and then looked back to his papers. John Paine rolled his eyes; it had been a long night, a long six months, in fact, and it was now being prolonged this little bit more by the CIA station chief, a man who had never been on the sharp end of things.

They waited a minute or two while Cannon studied the document he held in his hand. It took him so long to read it that Paine could only marvel at what must be the slowest reading speed in the entire agency.

Cannon was CIA aristocracy. His grandfather had been a friend and adviser to presidents, his father an old pal of Wild Bill Donovan, the founder of the OSS back in World War II and the father of the modern CIA. Hanging on the wall behind Cannon were pictures, Cannon *pere et fils* with Donovan, Allen Dulles, the first director of the CIA, legendary superspook James Jesus Angleton, a clutch of presidents, and later directors of Central Intelligence; naturally there was a Yale diploma hanging on the wall too, proudly announcing that Paulus Cannonus was the holder of a B.A. magna cum laude from that famous CIA spawning ground. Paine wondered why Cannon didn't have a framed, notorized certificate of his net worth too, a diploma testifying to the enormous inheritance that had come his way when his father had died, leaving him the Cannon millions—after all, private wealth, along with the Yale diploma and the

Skull and Bones membership, was part of the CIA aristocrat's makeup.

Cannon put down his file and smiled pleasantly at the two men. "Six compound fractures of the ribs," he said, as if he were remarking on the weather, "and a broken jaw." He looked back to his file. "Severe contusion of the groin and seven compressed vertebrae," he continued. "And that is only a preliminary report. My goodness, Mr. Paine, you do fight to win, don't you?"

"I'm terribly sorry, Mr. Cannon. I was trying to be careful. However, on my way home I planned to send them flowers and a basket of fruit."

"Ha ha," said Cannon. "Always the joker."

"Laughter is the best medicine, Mr. Cannon."

Cannon dropped his smile. "Okay, let's cut the crap here, Paine. You've paralyzed one of those kids, and the other is going to have to have his jaw wired together for six months. Not that I give a shit about them; it just makes interrogation a little harder. Your instructions were to deliver them more or less intact."

"And they are, the way I see it, more or less intact."

"Still alive, you mean."

"It's something."

"You would have, no doubt, preferred to have killed them."

"No," said Paine, "I did not see it that way."

"You will see things the way you are told to see them, Paine."

John Paine shrugged. "Is that all, Mr. Cannon?"

"No, that is not all. I just want to remind you that you are under my jurisdiction while you are operating in Italy, and what I say goes. I don't approve of Langley having dumped you on me. I don't like having free agents operating in my section; you go-anywhere, do-anything types rock the boat. You get the allies upset. If you had killed one of those men tonight, I would have been up to my neck in shit explaining the whole thing to the Italians. Now, I know that a certain amount of violence is involved in what you do, and as I say, I don't mind your meting out a little punishment to sworn enemies of the United States, but I will not have this kind of wanton brutality."

Paine flashed on an image of himself kneeling at Ali Akbar Mahoud's feet and wondered, if he had received a bullet in the brain, whether Cannon would have classified that as an amount of violence.

"Do you understand me, Paine?" Cannon sounded like a headmaster reprimanding a prep school boy for being caught smoking.

"That's a clip-on bow tie, isn't it?"

Cannon tossed the papers down on his desk. "Walter, get him out of here."

Hapgood and Paine didn't speak until they were out on the Via Veneto again.

"Boy, John, you just can't keep your mouth shut, can you?"

"Walter, give me a break, please..." Paine could feel the bands of fatigue tightening across his shoulders.

"No, goddammit, you give yourself a break. Cannon is going places in the Agency; hell, he'll probably be DCI someday—"

"That's when I'll go see what my services are worth to Syria."

"John, don't even joke about stuff like that. You've got too much time invested in this to blow it now."

The two men were walking down the Via Veneto toward the Piazza Barberini. The first signs of dawn were appearing in the eastern sky, giving the domes of the city a gray glow. The sparrows in the trees that lined the street were just coming out, preparing for a busy day of chirping and shitting on passersby.

In the Piazza, a café was setting up, ready for the early morning traffic of whores, transvestites, bus drivers, and off-duty cops. The tantalizing smell of fresh, strong coffee wafted out into the cool morning air.

"C'mon," said Hapgood, "I'll buy you a cup of coffee."

"Walter, I'm just going to head home..."

"It'll do you good," said Hapgood, steering him into the café.

They stood at the aluminum bar, Hapgood drinking a sweet cappuccino while Paine sipped a bitter *caffè ristretto*, feeling the caffeine kicking in almost at once.

"Look," said Hapgood, "Cannon's an asshole; we all know that. Speaking for myself, I want to say that you've done a hell of a job, setting up the Winston cover and taking down those two pieces of shit."

"Darn it," said Paine in mock consternation, "I just wish I hadn't hurt them so bad."

"For Christ's sake, John, stop feeling sorry for yourself."

"I'm not," said Paine. "I just think it's a little ironic that we have two PFLP members in custody and I'm warned about the excessive use of force. Doesn't that strike you as a little strange?"

"You know what the hell's going on. Cannon is just plain jealous. You thought up the plan, you set the trap, you sprung it, and Cannon looks like a desk pilot—"

"Who will, no doubt, take the credit."

Hapgood laughed. "When was the last time you cared about who got the credit?"

"I don't give a damn about it for me. I just don't want him to get it." Paine smiled. "It reminds me a little of some operations I did in a small Southeast Asian country. What was it called? Begins with a V . . ."

Hapgood shook his head. "Yeah, if you ask me, all your trouble began in a small Southeast Asian country that begins with V. You Phoenix Program types thought you were a law unto yourselves. You charged around Nam like the avenging angel knocking off VC leaders and NV generals, and you know what the problem with that was?"

"No, Walt, tell me."

"You fucking *enjoyed* it."

"No," said Paine, "I didn't enjoy killing VC and North Vietnamese. What I enjoyed was killing ARVN."

Hapgood threw his hands in the air. "You see what I mean? The ARVN were supposed to be our allies..."

"With the operative word being 'supposed.' You know who else was supposed to be on our side?"

"Australia?"

"Apart from them."

"Who?"

"MACV, Military Assistance Command, Vietnam. And you know who else? The State Department. And you know who else? Langley. Christ, Langley set up the Phoenix Program. We found a piece of shit ARVN colonel who had set himself up like a warlord"—Paine shook his head—"I forget where, could have been Quang Tri; I don't remember. He went in for the usual shit, selling matériel to the VC, but then he got a great idea. He would wait until there was a North Vietnamese regular battalion working in his district, make contact, and make a deal. He'd call in an air strike to get rid of them, but the enemy had already, mysteriously, found out the coordinates, the IP, the time down to the minute of the run, and guess what? The regulars were

28

waiting, and they blew those poor shits out of the sky. And you know why? For aluminum." Paine slapped the bar. "That ARVN colonel was selling scrap metal to the North Vietnamese, delivered. They would shoot down the planes and then strip them, carry the scrap up the Trail to Hanoi."

"John, it was a shitty little war . . ."

"He was a shitty little colonel in the Army of the Republic of Vietnam," said Paine evenly, "and when I killed him, yes, I enjoyed it."

"So you had your kicks."

"For a minute or two, it was satisfying. Until I got pulled out, sent back to Saigon, and informed that the execution had not been 'expedient.' It seems that my colonel was related to whichever tinhorn dictator we were supporting at the moment."

"That doesn't explain why now, twenty years later, you're acting like the whole world is against you."

"Not the whole world, just my own side. The rear echelon types like Cannon who don't approve of 'violence.'"

"You came out of it okay."

"A lot of people didn't."

"Let me guess; now you're going to start in about Kevin Cunningham, right?"

"I might."

"Cunningham is okay now. Christ, he's still with the Agency."

"What's left of him is still with the Agency."

"He stepped on a mine, John; it was a *war*."

"He stepped on one of our mines. A mine that wasn't supposed to be there, a mine that G-Two said wasn't there. That never *had* been there. But let me tell you, it was there, and I know, because I was there too."

Cunningham and Paine had been legendary operatives in the Phoenix Program, twenty-year-old kids with brains, balls, and steel where their nerves were supposed to be. They had both been accorded the rare privilege of being hated by both sides and were accordingly honored: the crooked ARVN officers, the VC, and the North Vietnamese had all put prices on their heads. When Cunningham and Paine had been led into that trap near Kontum, Cunningham lost both legs and most of one arm. Paine had carried his friend on his back, covering thirty miles of hard country, into a more or less safe sector, before calling in American medivacs. As soon as Cunningham was safely on board a Saigon-bound helicopter, Paine had disappeared, melting into the countryside for three weeks conducting a personal war, three-sided, against the ARVN, the VC, and the North Vietnamese regulars, anyone he suspected of having set him up. Intelligence reported a considerable softening of resolve in the sector, and when Paine came out, the Air Cavalry went in, and a victory for the side of truth and right and justice was declared.

Paine claimed that he had been disoriented and down with malaria for three weeks and denied any knowledge of military action in the region. The Army and the CIA couldn't decide whether to give him the Silver Star, court-martial him, or both.

Cunningham lived and took a job at Langley. Paine stayed on the outside, working in Vietnam until 1975, long after American ground troops were officially withdrawn. There were still some people in Washington who remembered Paine and what became known as the "Kontum caper," and protected him. It was the kind of esteem that pictures of Dulles and a Yale diploma could never earn.

Hapgood sighed heavily. "The hell with it, I'm beat." He drained his coffee.

"Have a nice day, Walter," Paine said sardonically, and left him in the bar.

John Paine walked home, enjoying the morning air and the sheer beauty of the city, which still dozed. He threaded his way through the narrow old streets, passing on every corner, it seemed, a noble church or magnificent palace. It was a city he loved, above all others, but he had never been completely seduced by its charms. Paine knew its history and it sobered him; every palace was built on a foundation of corruption and treachery, a legacy of Rome's violent past; for every church there was a betrayal, for every grand monument, a dark shadow of evil.

His apartment was in the oldest part of the city, in the *rione* of Monti, a slum in the days of ancient Rome with a seething populace capable of bringing down an emperor; as a young man, no less a personage than Julius Caesar, then just an up-and-coming army officer, had lived in those crowded streets. Today it was the home of the proud *Monticiani*, a neighborhood that had resisted the gentrification of the rest of the city; the Monticiani arrogantly claimed that they, and they alone, were the real Romans.

Signora Giusippina, the grumpy *portiera*, the doorkeeper of Paine's shabby apartment building on the Via Baccina, barely nodded to him as he walked into the building; you didn't merit the signora's esteem unless you had been born in the narrow streets bordered by the Via Cavour and the Via Nazionale. Paine was considered *simpàtico* by most, but he would always be an outsider.

He chuckled to himself as he climbed the steep stairs to his small top-floor apartment. It was his ambition in life to win Signora Guisippina's respect, and he knew it was one battle he was going to lose.

As he put the key in the lock of the reinforced door of his apartment, he could hear the phone ringing within. He hurried to answer it, catching it on the sixth ring. As he lifted the receiver, he could hear the little intercontinental squeak, a sign that it was a call from far away. For a moment there was nothing but hazy static on the line, then a voice, soft and indistinct, mumbling words that Paine had to strain to hear.

"My son will be early," said the voice. "Please arrange to have the driver notified."

"Of course," replied Paine. "When can we expect him?"

"Within the hour, perhaps sooner." Then the connection was broken.

Paine put down the phone and left the apartment, hurrying out into the sunny city, sleep delayed for hours to come.

3

Paine raced across town to the international telephone center housed in the Rome central post office in the busy, traffic-choked Piazza San Silvestro. The clock on the facade of the building showed 7:00 A.M., and the telephone exchange was deserted. The busy time would come later in the day as tourists, recently relieved of their wallets and purses by pickpockets, would line up for hours waiting for the chance to phone home, report the disaster, and arrange for emergency cash and cancel their credit cards.

Paine gave a number to the woman behind the desk, and she assigned him a booth. He locked himself into the soundproof chamber and dialed a number beginning with the prefix 0098 followed by 21; 0098 was the international code for Iran, and 21 for the city of Tehran.

His call was answered on the second ring, but whoever picked up the receiver didn't speak. Paine paused a moment, then said:

"Hotel Intercontinental?"

Someone whispered something, then there was the sound of the phone being passed from one hand to another.

"Yes?" demanded a voice in English.

"Hotel Intercontinental?" Paine repeated.

"Yes."

Paine nodded to himself and put down the phone. He left the booth and paid two thousand lire for the call at the cashier's desk. The woman behind the desk hardly glanced at him and didn't notice the fine sweat that had broken out on his brow.

Paine left the building and walked briskly up the Via del Tritone, looking like a slightly disheveled businessman anxious to beat the commuter rush. Within, though, his brain had slipped into high gear. The call at his apartment had been a cry for help from an operative in Tehran; the line had been bad, but he thought he recognized the voice of Dr. Tabriz, an agent-in-place, carefully hidden within the Iranian Foreign Ministry. Paine's return call told the whole story. If Tabriz were out of danger, he would have answered Paine's request for the Hotel Intercontinental simply, claiming that Paine had reached a wrong number. There was no code-work that required the answerer to respond in the affirmative. Tabriz had been picked up, and his apartment was probably at that moment being ransacked by Revolutionary Guards. Something bad had happened, and

Paine could only pray that Tabriz had managed to get away, or had been killed already—he held the key to the Tehran ring, known as Coyote 1.

The Marine at the Embassy desk informed him that Paul Cannon was still in the building, and the CIA duty officer told him that Cannon could be found in the cafeteria in the basement of the building.

Cannon was seated alone at one of the tables eating a plate of bacon and eggs and reading that day's edition of the *London Financial Times*, the pink of the newsprint almost the same hue as Cannon's babylike skin. He was rooting around in the stock market prices, trying to find out how his ICI shares had done overnight. He looked up from the tiny print as Paine took the seat across from him. Cannon frowned in displeasure.

"What do you want?"

They were seated far from the next occupied table, but Paine spoke in a whisper anyway.

"I just heard from Coyote One."

Cannon winced. "Jesus Christ."

For once, Paine and Cannon were in agreement. "My feelings exactly."

"What happened?"

"Not here," said Paine. "Upstairs."

The secure vault on the CIA floor was a room within a room. It had been built by technicians specially imported from the United States, a soundproof steel cell which could repel every type of listening device known to the Agency.

Rome was a major intelligence crossroad, a listening post on the Middle East and the potentially hostile governments of southern Europe and North Africa—the Russians, the Syrians, and the Libyans. Even friendly governments like Britain, West Germany, and France, not to mention Italy, were all very curious to know what was discussed in the Agency headquarters for the region. The vault was designed to thwart such eavesdropping, though that didn't stop the entire building from being bombarded with microwaves twenty-four hours a day in the hope that listening equipment could pick up something. Paine was no expert on that high-tech side of things, but he preferred to conduct his business in the inner sanctum, just to be on the safe side.

The ride up to the third floor had given Cannon time to compose himself. By the time they were settled in the vault, he had reassumed his headmasterish demeanor.

"What the hell was Coyote One doing calling you, at home?"

"He was desperate."

"Damn desperate. But why the hell you?"

Paine looked coolly at Cannon. "Because he trusts me."

"You're not the caseworker."

"I put him in place."

"That's no excuse."

"I'm sure he regrets not going through the

proper channels. I'm sure it's weighing heavily on his mind right now."

"Don't get sarcastic with me, Paine." Cannon swept a hand through his thinning blond hair. "You're sure it wasn't a plant?"

"No, you can never be sure of that. Besides, even if it was, then Coyote One is down. They got the information, and if that wasn't Tabriz, they want to provoke us into doing something, bringing the rest of the circle in. I'm pretty sure it was Tabriz, though."

"Damn," said Cannon. Coyote 1 was a golden and perfectly functioning spy ring in the heart of the most anti-American government in the world. The intelligence it had generated had been class-one, always accurate, never any garbage, and it had been operating for seven years, through the worst of the Khomeini era; Coyote 1 was so secret that the actual makeup of the band was known only to a handful of people; the top Iran analysts and the White House didn't know the source of the intelligence— which was just as well, Paine figured, because if North and Secord and the rest of the Iran Contra clowns had known about it, they would have been sure to blow it.

In the chain of command, Paine was the lowest-ranking member of the Agency to know the makeup of Coyote 1. Cannon had to know about it because he was the nominal control and there were probably only seven or eight officers at Langley in the know. The DCI, a political appointee, only knew what he had to know.

"Shit," blurted Cannon. "What the hell are they going to say in Langley?"

"Right now that's not what worries me."

"Really? What's on your mind, Paine?"

"Tabriz and the rest of them, in Tehran."

"They're gone," Cannon said curtly. "We have to assume they're gone until we can confirm otherwise."

Paine's face darkened. "That's it. A shrug of the shoulders and walk away. Too bad, Coyote One. That's the way the cookie crumbles."

A red light went on over the steel door of the vault. Cannon pressed a button on the table in front of him and the door clicked open. Hapgood pushed open the door—it was as thick and as heavy as the door of an industrial deep freeze—and rushed in.

"We're getting signals from the Sixth Fleet, Paul. Seems like something big is up in Tehran."

Cannon nodded at Paine. "We know already. Walter, it looks like we've lost Coyote One."

Paine looked quizzically at Hapgood. "You're cleared for that?"

"I'm second-in-command chief of station, John; what the hell do you think?"

Paine shook his head wearily. Walter Hapgood could be trusted with a secret, but how far along the line had the information gone?

"Besides," said Cannon, "by this afternoon the whole world will know."

"And State will release a statement claiming the whole thing to be all in Tehran's overheated imagination. And tomorrow everyone will have forgotten about it."

"Except for Tabriz and the rest. They'll have a long time to think about it while they're hanging by their thumbs in a meat locker somewhere in Iran."

"So what do you want? You want to get greased up and charge in there and rescue them? What the hell have you become, John? You know how the game works, and they know."

"Coyote One was self-contained. They'll only bring down one ring," said Cannon, already working out the extent of the downside.

"How the hell could it happen?" demanded Paine. "They were dead-hand. No one could have found them unless they knew where to look. The material they supplied was always backgrounded, never used up front by State, by us, by the White House."

"You know how it is," said Hapgood. "Someone got careless."

"After seven years?"

"It happens."

Not in operations I set up, thought Paine. "So now what?"

"Don't worry about it," said Cannon blithely.

Paine felt his jaw clench. "That's all you've got to say? 'Don't worry about it'?"

"Oh yeah, don't worry about it and get a couple of Cobras in the air so Mr. John Paine can fly over to Tehran and spring his buddies. Act your age, for Christ's sake."

"Anyway, John," said Hapgood, "about the thing last night—"

The simple operation of the night before seemed to Paine as if it had happened years ago. He could hardly remember the kid's face now or the name of the barman at the Club Paradiso.

"The kid is talking—it's not easy for him, but he's talking. Seems like they had something planned for a U.S. carrier out of Rome. Pan Am, TWA, just like flight 103 in eighty-eight. You can credit yourself with stopping that at least."

"The Lord giveth and the Lord taketh away," said Cannon without a hint of irony.

Paine got wearily to his feet. He was due at the office at the Food and Agriculture Organization. Jerry Winston couldn't disappear just yet: he had another week of the charade before Winston could be transferred back to New York and the "home office."

Cannon raised his hand. "Not so fast, Paine."

Paine sat down again. "What?"

"You're on your way to Berlin."

"What for?"

"I have no idea. All I know is that I got a signal for you to head to Berlin. You've been booked on a Swissair flight to Zurich at ten-thirty. You connect to Lufthansa and get to Berlin at two thirty-five."

"What about Winston?"

"That's been taken care of."

"And Coyote One?"

"It's in capable hands."

"And I'm supposed to go to Berlin for some other bullshit operation? Why me? Why can't Berlin station handle whatever it is they've got set up?"

"You'll have to take that up in Berlin, Paine."

"This is ridiculous. I spend six months setting up the Winston thing, Coyote One gets wrecked, and all of a sudden I'm supposed to head to Berlin like I was a traveling salesman?"

"Tired, Paine? Feeling the age a little, maybe?"

"Don't bait me, Cannon."

Paul Cannon was silent a moment, wondering if he had the courage to rebuke his subordinate for insolence. He decided on the easy way out. The headmaster returned.

"You are assigned, Paine. See Sam Grove in Berlin." Cannon stood up. "And let me say how glad I am that you're his problem for a while."

Hapgood tightened his tie and waited nervously for Cannon to leave the vault. Once he had gone, he turned to Paine, looking sorrowful.

"Just can't learn to keep that mouth shut, can you?"

Paine stood up. "You know, Wally, if I didn't know any better, I would say Cannon was trying to get rid of me."

"Jeez, whatever gave you that idea?"

"Just a hunch, Mr. Hapgood."

Paine returned to his apartment, showered,

shaved, and looked longingly at his bed. But he knew he didn't have time for a nap, and he told himself he could sleep on the plane. He did allow himself the luxury of a cup of coffee, which he made and took outside to his small terrace, which overlooked the imperial forum. He sipped the scalding brew as he watched the tourists wander around the ruins, marveling at the grandeur of ancient Rome. For a moment, Paine envied them: ordinary people with ordinary jobs who had taken a few days out of their ordinary lives for a look at Rome. For them, staying in a hotel was a luxury, eating in a restaurant was a thrill. Air-conditioned tour buses swept them around the city, telling what to look at, what to admire, what to think, eat, drink, and buy. So simple.

Paine hated air travel, restaurants bored him, and hotels, no matter how luxurious, smacked of loneliness and despair. In the last year he had been in a hundred cities all over the globe, ancient cities, heavy with the weight of history, or bustling, modern, vibrant cities, cities of the future, and in not one of them had he seen a sight, tasted the life. His travel was a never-ending cycle of meetings, whispered talks with shadowy men in anonymous suburbs, punctuated with moments of violence like the night before.

He remembered the first time he had come to Rome, scrambling over the ruins with his Blue Guide in hand, hoping to submerge his recent past—he had just left Vietnam—under the heavy press of centuries past. But he hadn't succeeded. When he happened on a "chance" meeting with Walter Hapgood in a little restaurant in Testaccio, he allowed himself to go for the bait, swallowing the CIA line and letting himself be reeled in, back into the choppy waters of the Agency ocean.

At the time, he remembered something Kevin Cunningham had said to him once after they emerged from some VC underground labyrinths they had just cleaned out with some of the fearless Vietnam tunnel rats. They were bloody and hurt and bone-tired; the wash of adrenaline sweeping out of them letting them down after the fast-pulse of danger.

"Jack," said Kevin Cunningham, "after this, the real world is going to be a mighty strange place."

4

It always struck Paine that in Berlin you could see the past and the present simultaneously. The city was still governed under rules enacted in 1945; the four powers still held their sectors and ran patrols in and out of each other's real estate just as they had when the city fell, acting as if the war had just ended. Berliners were still, technically, a subject people, liable to arrest without warrant, preventive detention, curfew, and censorship. They could be arrested for possession of weapons, and that meant something as innocent as a long-bladed kitchen knife. It was, as far as Paine knew, the only city in the world, outside of France, where anyone paid any attention to what the French thought; their patrols and checkpoints were just as rigorous as the American and the Russian; the British, thoughtfully, had toned down their military swagger.

In the present, however, was the real Berlin,

populated by hard-faced, hardworking Berliners, who put up with all this nonsense, the way adults ignore children playing cowboys and indians underfoot. It was only in the minds of the four powers that Berlin was still an occupied city. The Berliners didn't see it that way.

Berlin was also the only town in the world where espionage was a full-time, round-the-clock, night-shift-day-shift industry. Just as corporations had to have outposts in certain parts of the world if they were to be taken seriously, so intelligence services had to have a Berlin branch if they were to be seen as anything but lightweight. Chasing about both sides of the wall you could find operatives not just of the four powers but of smaller, less important countries as well. The last time Paine had been in Berlin, the American net had pulled in a member of the Ethiopian secret service—just what he was doing there, no one ever discovered or cared; he was just fouling the lines. He was expelled.

There just wasn't enough intelligence to go around. Every branch of American, French, Russian, and British espionage was represented in the divided city, a whole slew of initials: CIA, GRU, KGB, MI 5, 6, and 13, DST, SDCE, DIA, NIA. And each had its own jealously guarded patch of operation, its own operatives, informers, and strongmen. Sometimes Paine felt you couldn't walk down the street in Berlin without tripping over a spook. It was a wonder there was any room left for ordinary Berliners.

The CIA operations unit, not to be confused with the more cerebral CIA command in the consulate, was based in a modern office building off the Ku-dam, and inside looked much like the offices of an investment bank or a business consultancy. The front door was a little more secure than those of its innocent neighbors on the eleventh floor, and the receptionist, a pretty German woman, knew how to use the double-barreled shotgun clipped under her desk. In keeping with a number of other offices in the building, the CIA operations unit had music piped in. The difference was that the speakers were stuck to all the windows, oily Muzak pooling on the glass to interfere with the parabolic microphones that were pointed at the building. Paine couldn't help but feel sorry for the East German listeners who had to undergo hours of massed violins playing "The Shadow of Your Smile," in the hope of picking up a stray CIA secret.

The best thing about the CIA station in Berlin was its chief, Sam Grove. He was way past retirement, a scarred old war-horse, a veteran of a thousand operations starting with the old OSS days. He spoke half a dozen languages and seemed to know everybody everywhere, but unlike Cannon, he was not CIA aristocracy—his suits were too loud, his manner too abrasive, and far from not having gone to the right schools, he hadn't gone to school at all, at least, not after the sixth grade. Paine had never met a theatrical agent, but he always imagined that they were not unlike Sam Grove.

He looked out of place in his sleek designer office. The polished black marble desk and Sam Grove's rumpled figure just didn't match. The tasteful prints on the wall looked as if they had been chosen by a machine, and the black leather and chrome couch and chairs were better suited to an advertising agency whiz kid who had just achieved a career breakthrough as a result of some wonderfully clever new technique for the advertising of something nobody needed.

Sam Grove jumped to his feet as Paine was shown in. He was short and bald and chunky, like a bulldog, not conforming to the slim, tall, patrician type that the CIA liked to think of as the template for the perfect officer.

"Johnny Paine, how the fuck are ya?" You could take Sam Grove out of the Bronx, but you could never take the Bronx out of his voice.

"Just fine, Sam. You?"

"Great. Just had a bypass."

"I didn't know that."

"Eh," said Sam dismissively. "Do you know Mr. Wilson, here? He's Langley technical."

Wilson was a youngish man with prematurely white hair, a damp palm, and a squishy handshake. He pushed back his black-framed glasses and peered at John Paine, as if he were the first field agent he had seen close up.

"How do you do, Mr. Paine."

"Coffee, Johnny?"

Berlin coffee was almost as good as Italian. "Sure."

"Wilson?"

"Yes, please." Grove pressed a button on his desk and a secretary appeared with a tray and two cups of coffee.

"*Schlag?*" she asked Wilson.

"I'm sorry?"

"Yeah, what the hell, dump some in there, Helen," ordered Grove. The secretary spooned some heavy cream into Wilson's cup. Grove looked wistfully at the coffee and cream. "I'm not allowed, you know." He tapped his chest. "No booze, no cigars, nothing."

"That's too bad, Sam."

"Eh," he said again. "It's funny how you don't miss that stuff if it means you get to stay alive a little longer."

"That's a good way of looking at it."

"Eh. Helen, ask Charlie Sullivan to come in here when he gets a chance."

"Yes, Mr. Grove."

When Helen left, Sam Grove got down to business immediately. "So, Johnny, you're working here for a couple of days."

"Doing what?"

"You're hand-holding."

"Wonderful," Paine muttered without enthusiasm. "Am I going over?"

"Of course. If it was hand-holding on this side, I coulda got anybody to do it."

"You could probably still get anybody to do it."

"That's right. But the music goes round and round and it came up you. Don't ask me why."

Wilson cleared his throat tentatively. "Well, Mr. Paine, the decision was taken at Langley, actually. It seemed that you would be best suited to this operation."

"How is that?"

"Certain characteristics in your background, Mr. Paine, and the fact that you haven't worked here in some years. It was decided that a Berlin operative would be too conspicuous."

"In other words, Johnny, you're cold and you kill."

Paine frowned. "And who gets killed?"

"Well," said Wilson, "we hope no one, but should the circumstances arise . . ."

Grove, characteristically, cut through the crap. "You've got to go pick up a scientist"—he snapped his fingers at Wilson—"what's his name?"

"Halbach, Mr. Grove, Dieter Halbach."

"And what's his specialty?"

"Artificial coenzymes, Mr. Grove. He's a biophysicist."

"Whatever," said Grove. "Anyway, he wants to come out and we want him out, and so you have to get him." Grove stopped, and for a moment, his attention wandered, as if he was thinking of the good old days when he was working behind enemy lines or subverting a government somewhere, not worrying about artificial coenzymes.

"I still don't get it, Sam. Why me?"

"Because that's what the big bosses want. That should be good enough, Johnny."

It wasn't, but Paine knew that was all he was going to get. "Fine."

"Good."

"Perhaps, Mr. Grove, you should tell Mr. Paine that—"

"Yeah, don't rush me, Wilson. You're taking Wilson here over with you."

Paine swung around and looked at the lanky young man. He had U.S. of A. stamped all over him, and looked as if he'd break in a moderately high wind. "I am?"

"Yeah."

"Why?"

"Always with the questions, Johnny."

"I have been asked to meet with Halbach before he comes over, to evaluate some data and a physical plant. Something that can only be done in situ."

Paine was not happy. "And where's the situ?"

"Furstenwalde; know it?"

Paine relaxed a little. Furstenwalde wasn't too bad; it was only fifty or sixty kilometers into the East, so he wouldn't have to travel far; on the other hand, the closer things were to the border, the better-guarded they were.

"There's a biomedical research center in Furstenwalde where this Halbach guy works.

Lucky for us, it's right on the Spee, or rather, a canal off the river. The idea is that you float in, Mr. Wilson looks at some, I dunno, some scientific shit, and then you, Wilson, and Halbach float out. You have to make sure that they both get here alive."

Wilson gulped.

"What do I float in on?"

"A barge. Charlie will be here in a minute; he'll tell you all you need to know."

Except why me, thought Paine. "I don't mean to insult you, Mr. Wilson—"

"Al, please."

"Al. But I'm not sure you're quite up to—"

"Um, well, I was in the Army."

"That a fact?"

"Yes. It was research at Fort Ben Harrison, but I did basic like everybody else."

Well, that changes everything, thought Paine sourly.

"Johnny-boy, sorry, but it's decided and you can't change it. Please don't rock the boat."

"Barge," said Wilson with a grin.

"Good one," said Grove.

Charlie Sullivan was chief of operations for CIA station Berlin. He slipped into the office holding a folder, nodded at Paine and Wilson, and ignored Grove. The two men didn't get on, although there was no single bone of contention. They just rubbed each other the wrong way. Still, they had been working together, side by side, year after year, with nary a hitch.

"How's your German, Paine?"

"Fair."

"Then try not to say much."

"I always try."

"But don't always succeed," cackled Grove.

Sullivan looked at his chief with contempt. "There is a barge on the Spee here in the West; it's been traveling in and out of the East for years, run by our friends and allies the West Germans. They've never had any trouble."

"How many? In the crew, I mean."

"Four. Skipper—he's professional—first mate, and two deckhands. They're just kids. They carry gravel from West to East and lumber from East to West. Good hiding on both ends of the trip. The Vopo would have to be pretty good—they'd have to take the barge apart—to find the bolt holes. I've got papers for you and Wilson—you speak German, Wilson?"

"Ah, yes, sir, I do. Most of the major texts in my field are written in—"

"Good."

"You're going in tonight. You should be out tomorrow by this time, I'd say." Sullivan tossed the file at Paine. "Read this, then return it to research. We've got some suitable clothes for you too. Come back here at ten and we'll go over things, get you suited up and down to the barge. Got it?"

Paine nodded. "Weapons?"

"There's some on the boat, but you won't be

carrying anything personally. Please try and avoid trouble, Paine. Things are nice and quiet here right now. Glasnost and perestroika, you know."

"Eh," said Grove.

The briefing folder that Sullivan gave Paine didn't tell him much more than he knew already. On paper, the operation looked pretty simple, but then, they always did. Halbach was one of those rare defectors who was coming over not for financial or ideological reasons, but for scientific motives. He had gone as far as he could in his native country—there just wasn't enough money to fund his research in East Germany, and no one seemed to appreciate just how valuable his work was. Neither did Paine: there was a long technological note explaining just what artificial coenzymes were, but he skipped it. He hoped that he could avoid the subject with Wilson as easily—"Al" looked as if he could wax poetic about whatever they were for a good two or three hours.

Paine returned the folder to research as instructed, then returned to his hotel and finally got some sleep. He had been up now for thirty-six hours, and he knew, on awakening, that he wasn't as sharp as he should be. He was sure that he was perfectly competent to attempt the mission, but the edge was missing, the extra alertness that a good agent took with him into the field. Things would just have to work his way and go as smoothly as they planned.

By eleven, he and Wilson were dressed in the crusty, filthy clothes of bargemen: heavy denim shirts, thick-soled boots, and overalls. Wilson had added a cap to the outfit, and he looked, in a word, ridiculous.

"Where are your glasses?" asked Paine.

"I've got contacts," said Wilson, blinking myopically.

"You sure you can see?"

"You bet." Paine could tell that the young man was excited, and why not? It probably made a nice change from whatever boring job it was that he did back in Virginia.

At ten minutes to midnight, they went aboard the barge. It was a dirty old hulk, but it rode easily on the oily river. There was a wheelhouse in the stern and then a long, straight keel piled high with gravel, and a rounded, blunt bow.

The captain was gruff, the way captains are supposed to be, and the mate and the two deckhands looked like young West Germans of a type you met everywhere these days. They argued continually about what kind of music to play on the cassette deck in the wheelhouse—Queen won—and before the barge shoved off, they were earnestly debating the merits of the Mercedes 190 against those of a BMW 320i. Paine knew he could not depend on them in case of trouble, but then, that wasn't their job. They had to run the boat and keep their mouths shut on serious matters. Better to leave them to their rock music and expensive automobiles.

The barge was only making three or four knots as it coasted up to the West German marine border point. A British naval rating came aboard, glanced at the papers and at the crew, stamped the log. The formalities on the East German side were hardly more elaborate. The captain knew the customs man, and they chatted about soccer while the appropriate rubber stamp slammed down on two sets of transport forms.

At twelve-thirty the great iron doors of the first lock on the Spee opened for the barge. At that point on the river, there was a set of rapids, very popular with white-water enthusiasts in the East, but too steep for a riverboat. The lock carried them around it. The doors shut with a clang, and the water level started to drop. Paine had never been in a canal lock before, and he wasn't sure he liked it. On either side of him rose the sheer walls of the chamber, and all he could see beyond that was a patch of night sky high above and the reflected light of the lockmaster's house.

It took about thirty minutes for the lock to drain. The set of iron doors on the far end of the lock started to swing open, sloshing a great bank of water against the prow. The boat slid over it, and the skipper boosted the throttle a little, nosing the long craft into the East German part of the river.

Paine glanced over at Al Wilson and saw the young man's eyes bright with excitement in the glow of the instruments on the bridge. Paine tried to remember how he had felt on his first trip into the East. He remembered vividly: he had been scared.

5

There was a lot of traffic on the river, and the captain stayed on the bridge all night, listening to the radio chatter from the other barges, regulating the wheel and throttles with the touch of a safecracker. The duties of the first mate didn't seem to be that onerous; he stood by the captain, peering into the night with a pair of binoculars, murmuring the names of the other ships they passed, making the identification by outline, not name. Once or twice the skipper got on the radio and chatted with one of the vessels, talking to other skippers he knew, asking about river conditions, weather, berthing upriver. Someone advised him of the location of a customs launch, but they motored by it, the officials not giving them a second glance.

The two deckhands didn't seem to do much besides make coffee and, in the depths of the night, bacon and eggs. Paine hadn't realized until they started serving how hungry he was. He wolfed down his portion and wished there were more; Al Wilson scarcely touched his.

They were ten or twelve miles into the East when the skipper of the barge turned to Paine.

"You've been over before?"

"Once or twice."

The captain smiled. "Not saying much, are you?"

Paine shrugged. If the captain was as professional as Sullivan claimed he was, then he should know that there wasn't much he could say.

"You know the country?"

"Parts of it. How about you? You know the lay of the land away from the river?"

The captain took a long time considering the question. "No, not anymore. It's all built over now. I haven't been a mile from the river for forty-four years."

Paine had guessed the man to be in his middle fifties, just young enough to have avoided fighting in the Second World War. Now, though, he reconsidered his judgment. "You from this area?"

The skipper shook his head. "No, Berlin. But I fought here. Or that's what they called it. More like a massacre. I was fifteen."

Paine knew the story. In the last days of Hitler's Germany, every available male was pressed into service. Children as young as the skipper had been then were given a gun and pointed east in the desperate hope that the youngsters could stop Stalin's army, battle-hardened Red Army veterans who had been fighting a savage war every day, year in, year out, since 1941. It was a pointless and pathetic waste of life. The last film shot of Hitler was a few minutes of footage of the Führer speaking to the children he was sending to their deaths. Strange, though, Paine recalled, in the grainy old film, Hitler had a look in his eye, a glimmer of hope that these children would be able to do the impossible.

"I had an old Mauser," said the captain, "six bullets, and a canteen. There were twenty, maybe twenty-five of us in the unit. Commanded by some old bastard who worked in the foreign ministry during the war. Never fired a shot before. We were about thirty kilometers from Furstenwalde when we ran into some Reds."

"And?"

"It was just a patrol. Eight or nine men. They didn't look like the monsters we had been told about. I gathered they were white Russians, you know; not the Asian variety. They looked like us."

"What happened?"

"We fired. I shot my six bullets and ran away. I guess the Russians killed the rest of them. I don't know. I never saw them again. Took me three days to get back to Berlin, but by that time my family had been bombed out." The captain broke off to snatch at the microphone of his shortwave; his call signal had come over the air.

It was nothing important, a friend in a passing barge that the captain had failed to see. The skipper got a good ribbing about being too old to be out at night if he didn't even recognize his old pal's ship . . . It was the usual radio joshing that men in professions like his indulged in.

Paine waited to see if the captain would resume his reminiscences. Presently he said: "You know, when a family got bombed out, after they found someplace else to live, if they were lucky enough, they'd go back to the ruins of their old house and put up a notice. You'd see them all over: Fritzi, I'm at such and such, Paulus, look for us at Auntie Zim's house, you know the kind of thing. The whole city was festooned with these little pieces of paper. My Mam never put up one for me. I guess she thought I'd never come back, or she died in the bombing." The captain touched the wheel, and the barge nudged to port. "They stopped digging out the bodies. No one had any strength, no tools. They were too busy trying to keep their heads down. I don't blame them. But you know, when I go to East Berlin to get my permits renewed, I get a funny feeling thinking that my whole family is buried under Karl Marx Strasse, maybe." The captain didn't look angry or sad. He spoke in a matter-of-fact voice. Paine must have shown that he noticed the skipper's apparent lack of concern. He smiled.

"Lots of worse things happened to other people in the war. And I don't just mean the Jews either. I lost my family—so, lots of people did. Berlin is used to that kind of thing. Next time you're walking down the Ku-dam and you see some woman in her fifties, sixties, seventies— and I don't care if she's buying bonbons at Ka-Di-Wa or sweeping the streets, I'll tell you something, if she was here in forty-five, she was raped—unless she was very lucky. Everyone suffered. It was a fact of life back then."

"That why you do this?"

"No." The captain shook his head curtly.

One of the deckhands, posted on the bow, ran nimbly back along the narrow decks and thrust his head into the bridge.

"Vopo," he hissed.

The captain put his hand on the throttle and gently eased back on the engines, slowing the vessel down. "You get below with the other one. Kurt will show you where."

Kurt, the boy from the bow, tugged at Paine's sleeve. "*Komm*," he whispered, as if the Volkspolizei, the Vopo, could hear him.

"What's going on?" asked Wilson, his Adam's apple bobbing up and down.

"We might be boarded by the local police."

"Jesus Christ!" Wilson's eyes were wide with alarm.

"It's routine. They're not looking for us."

Kurt pulled a piece of paneling off the wall of the cramped cabin, exposing what appeared to be a wall of gravel in the long hold of the

65

ship. But that too was false, a layer of gravel carefully glued onto a sheet of thin wood, pulled away to reveal a small space bored into the cargo, tight-packed stones on all sides.

Wilson almost dove into the hole, pulling his legs in after him. Paine could feel the ship slowing down, and across the water he could hear someone shouting to the barge captain through a loud-hailer. He squeezed in after Wilson, and Kurt slapped the false wall back in place, plunging the bolt hole into darkness. Paine felt like a rat caught in a trap.

The thrumming of the engine slowed a bit more, and Paine could not hear the panting, nervous breathing of his companion. He assumed that the captain had made some allowances for ventilation, but the air in the tiny space was damp and fetid; Wilson wasn't helping any either. The faster he breathed, the worse the air would become.

"Calm down," whispered Paine. "Try and control your breathing. Relax. Everything is going to be okay." Silently he cursed whoever it was who had arranged for him to be nursemaiding some Langley bookworm into the East.

Wilson fought to control himself. "I'm sorry. I'm just, well, I guess I'm a little claustrophobic."

Great, thought Paine. Wilson must have known that this was a possibility, and he hadn't told anyone he was afraid of confined spaces.

Paine prayed that Wilson didn't freak out when the police came aboard.

"Mr. Paine..."

"What?"

"You do have a weapon, don't you?"

"No."

"What!"

"Shuttup," ordered Paine. "A weapon would do no good here. Can't you see that?"

"Jesus Christ," muttered Wilson. "Oh, Jesus Christ."

Paine considered putting Wilson out with a carefully placed blow to the bone behind the ear, but there were two problems with that: He might seriously injure the young man, and he wasn't exactly sure where his head was. If he struck and missed, he was sure that Wilson would start screaming bloody murder and alert the whole damn river to their whereabouts. Better, he decided, to leave things as they were.

There was a gentle bump as the police launch came alongside the barge; then came the sound of the barge engines being throttled back. Paine couldn't hear the sound of voices in the wheelhouse, but he assumed that the Vopos were on board. He couldn't help but tense slightly, but tried to tell himself that the cops were just bored, going through the routine so they could show their superiors that they had been out on patrol making East Germany safe for socialism.

One thing was for certain. If they were discovered, then there was very little Paine could do about it. There would be no sense in trying to fight his way out—the cabin was sure to be filled with policemen bearing automatic weapons. It was no good being deadly, no use knowing how to kill a man in a thousand different ways, if half a dozen men had a gun on you.

Wilson seemed to be breathing easier now, having fought down his initial panic. Paine admired the young man for that: this was hardly the kind of thing he could be used to.

From beyond the false panel there came the sound of voices, muffled by the wood and gravel. Paine couldn't make out anything that was said, but he recognized the tone: bored, sleepy, going-through-the-motions officialdom.

He knew they were all right, but a few minutes later, as the panels were pulled away, he tensed, peering into the light, almost sure he would be looking down the barrel of a machine pistol. Instead he saw the face of Kurt, smiling happily.

"They're gone," he said.

Wilson surprised Paine. He was asleep, dreaming away in the tight space as if he were back in his comfy suburban bed in Arlington or Alexandria. It took a moment to wake him, and he acted a bit sheepish.

"My wife," he said with a nervous grin, "she does these yoga breathing exercises before she goes to bed. I've been watching her for five years and finally tonight I imitated her. Works like a charm."

"Thank God," said Paine. But something bothered him: the ability to calm yourself down, to reduce the heart rate and relax into a safe sleep, was something learned with great perseverance, not from watching your wife while you dozed over the late news.

Coffee was distributed all around in the wheelhouse. The captain seemed unfazed by his visit from the Vopos. He shrugged it off.

"Thirty years I've been on this river and they still don't know me, or they pretend not to. Every two or three trips they come aboard and look at my papers. Used to be more frequent when I used to give them coffee—almost every night, the bastards. Now I make sure that they don't get anything. Still, you can't blame them. Ever had coffee from the East?"

Paine nodded.

"Then you know why they stop us."

Paine chuckled. That was the East all over: use up a dozen gallons of diesel and a few hundred man-hours a week just so the late shift could have some decent coffee. Surely it would be cheaper just to buy some Nescafe?

"I should have told headquarters that we were due for a boarding, but I didn't want to upset anybody." He nodded toward Wilson.

"I'm sorry," said Wilson.

"You did fine."

Just before dawn, the barge eased into a berth in the Furstenwalde docks. Wilson and Paine hid in the gravel while the cargo was off-loaded—Paine would be interested to see how the hiding place was concealed after the tons of stones had been taken off. Wilson seemed better this time, used to the tight quarters, but he didn't fall asleep. Paine assumed that the last time, Wilson had been responding to a natural need; the body, disoriented and overwhelmed by fear, had just shut down, taking refuge in sleep. He had seen it a thousand times in combat, or just after. If Wilson wanted to believe that there was some mysterious Eastern, Tantric root to his behavior, then let him think that. Paine decided it had been a normal response to rank fear.

He guessed that they lay in port for about two or three hours; he estimated it was nine o'clock or thereabouts when the big diesel engines started up and the boat slipped out of port. The captain had already told him what would happen: They would head downriver to the lumber pier, passing, as they did so, Halbach's place of business. Once they had loaded up, they would steam upriver again, stop at the laboratories, and get down to business. In time, Paine, too, fell asleep, but from fatigue, not fear.

He was awakened by Kurt removing the cover from the secret hatch. There was a quiet whine coming from the engine room, indicating that the engines had been shut down; only the generator was operating, providing power to the ship.

"We are there," said Kurt.

"Have we taken on the lumber?"

"Yes," he said, and headed back up to the deck. It was a cold, damp morning, more like October than June, with a fine drizzle falling, a sticky rain that furred their clothes with a slick of tiny globules of water. Visibility on the river was poor, with a heavy mist screening the barge from the rest of the traffic. The shore was distinct for only a few yards inland. Beyond was the dim outline of some buildings, low and secretive-looking, dominated by a tall, thin shaft of a smokestack.

The captain and crew had the deck open, the floorboards pulled up to reveal the engines. The story was that the barge had encountered engine trouble and had put in at the lab dock to repair it. Oily tools lay scattered about, and the mate was down in the engine pit, his face streaked with grease. It looked convincing enough, and the skipper had taken the precaution of removing the rotator arm in case the Vopos came alongside and told him to fire the engines. It was a ruse that wouldn't hold up long, but it was something—and it was also "damage" quickly repaired if they had to get under way in a hurry.

"We have an hour, maybe a little less. We are in the radar sweep of the canal control at Furstenwalde. I've radioed that we're laid up here, so they'll be along eventually."

Paine was puzzled. If the authorities knew

71

that a barge was put up next to the laboratories, why weren't they on their way already? It was his experience that the powers in the East were very sensitive about Westerners camping out near their secret installations.

The skipper laughed, reading the meaning of the look on Paine's face. "Relax, my friend. This is a biology lab. Not defense. Sure, there's security, but not much."

Wilson looked at his watch. "I guess I better get going," he said nervously, like a boy about to go on his first date.

"Weapon?" Paine turned back to the skipper.

The captain looked doubtful. "I don't think that's a good idea. If you get caught, you can say you're a simple bargeman I sent ashore to look for some lubricating oil. If you've got a gun on you, that changes everything."

Paine could see the logic in that.

"There's a pistol clipped under the radarscope in the wheelhouse. You can take it if you'll feel better. But . . ."

Paine shrugged. "Never mind."

Paine and Wilson climbed up from the deck onto the dock, which towered above the barge. The pier was plainly meant to be used for larger vessels, but it was also obvious that it had not seen service in years. Weeds sprouted in the cracks in the concrete, and a single narrow-gauge railway line that ran along the pier had rusted over.

Sullivan's file said that Halbach would be

waiting in the warehouse at the end of the dock, a rusting corrugated iron structure that sagged on its foundations. It was dark inside and smelled of disuse and the muddy river.

The two Americans walked into the shed, Wilson blundering into the middle of the large, echoing room, Paine yanking him back into the shadows by the collar.

"You don't know who's in there," Paine hissed in his ear.

"Sorry, Mr. Paine."

Paine advanced cautiously, edging around the side of the room, toward a small office that had been built into one corner. He paused next to the sagging wooden door and listened. No sound.

He breathed deep and kicked, splintering the old planks. In a split second, he caught sight of not one but two men in the small room. And one of them had a gun.

6

Paine's first reaction, his instinctive gut response, was to attack, to neutralize the threat; but as he registered that thought, another came crowding into his brain—Wilson. If he got hurt, there would be hell to pay, and Paine could sense him standing in the doorway, an easy shot—you didn't have to be a marksman to drop him where he stood. Paine pirouetted and slammed Wilson to one side, knocking him to the floor. The young man went down, completely taken by surprise by the sudden attack.

"Stay down," ordered Paine. He sprung to his feet, wondering why he had not heard the sound of shots. The two Germans were standing in the doorway, both staring widemouthed at him. The one with the gun had not even raised it. The barrel was pointing toward the floor. Paine stopped, tensed.

"Good morning," stammered one of the Germans. Paine recognized him as Halbach.

"Who are you?" Paine demanded of the other, the one with the gun.

Wilson supplied the answer. "Professor Hartmann," he said, getting up from the dusty floor and extending his hand. "This is an honor indeed."

Professor Hartmann was in his fifties and looked faintly self-conscious about carrying a gun. Paine realized immediately what was going on: the gun had a cracked grip, and there was rust edging the barrel. It was an old, untrustworthy East bloc knockoff of a Colt, and it looked so untrustworthy that it would probably blow up in your hand. It was the kind of gun that Paine's old light weapons instructor used to say you were safer in front of than behind. The professors here, knowing that they were going to meet a couple of tough, battle-hardened American spooks, had decided that they needed some firepower for protection. Paine would have laughed if he hadn't been so annoyed. Someone could have gotten hurt—and if the Vopos had caught Hartmann carrying a gun, then they all would have gotten hurt.

Wilson, Halbach, and Hartmann were jabbering away in German, a technical side of the language that Paine couldn't begin to understand. Hartmann had a piece of paper out and he was explaining something to Wilson, while the American took notes in a tiny notebook. Halbach, much younger than his colleague, didn't say much, but kept glancing over at Paine as if he were the first American he had ever seen.

Bits and pieces of this cockeyed operation were beginning to fall into place. Wilson had said he had to come along on the journey to evaluate some data and the physical plant: Hartmann, who seemed to be senior to Halbach, was obviously both. Quietly Paine fumed; if Wilson and Sullivan had known that there was going to be a third party here, then they should have told him.

The three scientists talked nonstop for thirty minutes. Then Paine reminded them of the time; they talked for another ten until Paine insisted they be on their way.

Halbach, Hartmann, and Wilson exchanged a glance of impatience at Paine's scientific illiteracy.

"Wilson, let's go."

"Professor Hartmann should go first. It would be best for him to leave and go back to the lab. Then we should make our way down to the boat." Wilson was plainly concerned about the older man.

"No. We go first."

Wilson's face fell. "If you think that's best."

"I do."

Halbach and Hartmann showed unexpected emotion for Germans when they said their goodbyes. They embraced, like father and son, and Paine could have sworn that Hartmann had tears in his eyes.

"Take care of yourself, Dieter."

"*You* are the one who should be careful. I'm sorry for all the trouble that this will cause."

"Nonsense, my boy," said the older man. "It is for the good of science."

"Professor . . ." urged Paine.

Hartmann shook hands with Wilson. "It was an honor to meet you, sir," said the German. "I have admired your work for some time."

"The honor was all mine, Professor."

Paine rolled his eyes. "We have to move, Al. And I want absolute silence on the trip back to the barge. Do you understand?"

Both men nodded. They stole out into the gray gloom, walking in single file toward the riverbank. At the head of the dock, Paine motioned for them to stop while he moved forward. He could hear the muffled voices of the captain and crew on the ship, and no others. Things seemed to be all right.

"Captain?"

"*Ja?*"

"I couldn't find any oil," he called, hoping he sounded at least a little bit like a Berliner.

"That's all right," shouted the captain. "The river police came along and gave us some. Everything is working fine now."

That was as good an all clear as Paine was going to get. He motioned the two scientists forward, and together they scrambled down the rotting ladder into the barge. Five minutes later, they were under way, the long, slim boat carving a narrow passage in the mist.

Wilson and Halbach immediately went below and took up their scientific conversation where it had left off. Paine stayed on the bridge, watching the river through the spinner window, listening to the thrum of the engines and urging the barge forward. There was something about this mission that was getting on his nerves, the casualness of the scientists, as if they were meeting at some convention somewhere, rather than in enemy-held territory. When the captain wasn't looking, Paine felt under the radar scope, his hand closing around the handle of a revolver. Somehow that made him feel better.

"You had visitors while we were ashore?"

"Yes," said the captain, not taking his eyes off the prow of his vessel. "It was nothing."

"Are you sure?"

"Yes. Listen, my friend. To most people, the world is quite an innocent place. They don't see spies under every rock or on every old barge that happens to break down."

"The police, in my experience, tend to be quite suspicious of everything."

The captain smiled. "They are boys. Conscripts. I told you, they like West boats because sometimes they get a cup of coffee or a *Playboy* magazine. Relax."

"I'll do my best."

The barge chugged on, and soon Paine felt himself being lulled by the crackle of radio chatter and the hum of the engines. Still, he would be glad when this was all over, when he could return Wilson, in one piece, safe and sound, to Sam Grove and Sullivan. Of all the duty he could draw, hand-holding was the worst—you had to worry about other people, take care of them, rely on them. Paine had grown used to relying only on himself, ever since Cunningham had been half blown to pieces; he felt safer that way.

"We're two kilometers to the lock," said the captain after an hour or so of silence. "You better get them under wraps." He nodded toward the gangway that led down to the cabin. "There's not enough room in the hole for all three of you. One of you is going to have to stay on deck. I imagine that's going to be you."

"You imagine correctly."

"I thought so."

"How tough are they going out?"

"Depends who's on guard. If it's one of those officer types with the rule book memorized, they'll give us a little bit of a going over. If not..." The skipper shrugged. "Fifteen minutes, perhaps. Remember, for them, cargo going out means hard currency coming in. Never underestimate the power of Western money, particularly in a worker's paradise."

"What should I do?"

"Stand around and try to look as stupid as the rest of my crew. You're all right. You've got valid papers and passport. They couldn't stop you crossing if you started singing 'Yankee Doodle Dandy.' Besides, we have to clear the lock first, and the lockmaster will tell me who's on duty. At least we'll have a little warning..."

Halbach and Wilson were tucked away in their hiding place as the barge came up to the tall iron doors of the lock. The skipper and the lock controller talked on the radio for a moment, the control informing him that there was a ship on its way down; the barge would have to back down the river a ways and await the passage of the East-bound vessel, a delay of fifteen minutes.

Gradually the iron gates swung open and the needle nose of another West German barge edged out of the chamber, water swirling before it. The skipper saluted the passing vessel and received a toot from the passerby's horn.

"That's my brother-in-law," said the captain. "We won't even have to ask which lockmaster is on duty. They don't like it, you know. They do get a little suspicious." The captain unclipped the microphone and spoke to his brother-in-law. The answer jolted Paine, as sure as if he had put his hand in an electric socket.

"Hartmann," said the skipper's brother-in-law. "Hartmann is on duty, but he seems to be in a good mood. Waved us through without so much as a look-over. That's never happened before."

"I hope his mood keeps up," said the captain.

Hartmann? It was a common enough name in Germany, no matter which side of the wall you were on. It could not possibly be the same Hartmann he had seen just two hours earlier, tears in his eyes at the thought of losing a young colleague.

"What does Hartmann look like?" demanded Paine.

"Nothing very special about him," said the captain with a shrug. "Blond hair, pretty tall. Fifty-ish, I suppose."

That fit the description, but it also fit half the population of both Germanys, or half of Europe, for that matter. Paine wracked his brain trying to think of something distinctive about the scientist. There was nothing, nothing that set him apart. His voice; maybe he would recognize his voice.

"Is there any way you can get him on the radio, this Hartmann?" demanded Paine.

The skipper scowled. "Why in God's name would we want to do that? It would just raise his suspicions."

The captain was right, of course. "What about the Vopo channel? Can you tune it in, bring him up? Do you know the frequency?"

"Of course, but I have to keep tuned to the lock. It's regulations."

"I don't care. Just do it."

"Tell me what's going on."

"I think this is a trap."

The captain paled. "Oh God..."

Paine dashed down the companionway and pulled open the hiding place. "Halbach, get up here."

"What is happening?"

"Yeah, Mr. Paine, aren't we—"

"Just move." Paine grabbed Halbach roughly by the collar and dragged him halfway out of the hole. "Get up to the wheelhouse."

The gates of the lock were wide open now, and the skipper had received the go-ahead to bring his boat in.

"Slow," ordered Paine, "as slow as you can go." The captain barely touched the throttle, the boat easing forward almost imperceptibly. "Now change over to the Vopo channel." The captain turned the band selector and then looked to Paine for his next order.

"Kurt!" The deckhand came up into the wheelhouse. "Listen, I want you to do something for me."

"Yes, sir," said the boy, puzzled.

"Captain, what was the registration number of the river patrol boat that visited you when we were at the lab?"

The captain picked up a clipboard that hung below the instrument panel. "EC-twelve. Look, I've got to put this ship in the lock. I'll bet the master is screaming at me. I can almost hear him from here."

Paine thrust the microphone into Kurt's hand. The captain had said that those boats were manned by boys—young men like Kurt, probably. "Kurt, I want you to call Captain Hartmann and say you are the river patrol boat EC-twelve. Do you understand?"

Kurt nodded.

"Then do it."

Halbach looked pale. So did Wilson. "What's going on, Mr. Paine?"

Kurt looked to the captain. "Do it, Kurt; you've heard them enough times."

Kurt swallowed. "Here is patrol boat EC-twelve to the Berlin lock Volkspolizei, over."

The return was almost instantaneous. "Berlin lock go ahead."

"Ask for Hartmann. Say it's urgent."

"EC-twelve back to the lock, Captain Hartmann, over?"

"Berlin lock, stand by."

A tense minute passed. Then: "Here is Hartmann; go ahead, EC-twelve."

Paine turned to Halbach. "Is that him? Is that Professor Hartmann?"

"Here is Hartmann; go ahead."

"I . . ." stammered Halbach, "I can't be sure; on the radio, voices are different."

"Hartmann; go ahead." Hartmann sounded indignant. "Hartmann to EC-twelve, go ahead."

The radio crackled. "This is EC-twelve; identify yourself please."

The captain groaned. The real patrol boat, still in the waters, had picked up the signal. He swore under his breath.

"No," said Halbach suddenly, "that's not him."

"What the hell is going on here?" demanded Hartmann.

"EC-twelve to unit calling," said a very confused radioman.

"No, no, that's not him," insisted Halbach.

Suddenly Paine knew that it was. "Reverse engines!"

The captain almost fell over the throttles, shoving them back into full reverse. The big diesel engines screamed in annoyance at this rough treatment. For a second or two the barge sat immobile, the water boiling around it as the screws went from half ahead to full astern; then the blades caught and the boat lurched backward toward the closing lock gates.

The wheelhouse window disappeared, scattering chips of glass like shrapnel. Paine felt the sting as a handful of granules lacerated his cheek. Three East German soldiers had rappelled down the side of the lock, landing on the barge foredeck. They had hit the ground shooting. The first blast took out the window and the captain, who staggered back in the confined space, slammed against the rear wall, and collapsed, killed instantly by a head wound.

Paine dove for the floor, bringing Wilson and Halbach down with him. He grabbed under the radar scope pulling out the heavy revolver, and checking the clip in a single motion. It was a thirteen-shot Colt, a heavy weapon, which could cut a man in half if you got close in with it.

From the deck there was the sound of shooting and three high screams—the mate and the two deckhands, Paine figured. He guessed there were four, perhaps five soldiers on the cargo deck, two probably detailed to secure the ship, the other three sent in on the attack to take out the wheelhouse. There was one thing working in Paine's favor: He would have bet money that the soldiers had orders to take him, Wilson, and Halbach alive. Dead, they were a neat little package; alive, they were valuable for intelligence and propaganda purposes. He glanced over at Wilson, cowering in a corner of the cabin: he wouldn't last a minute if the East German security services got hold of him, less than that if he was handed over to the KGB.

Paine raised himself on one knee but was almost immediately thrown back to the deck. The barge, still traveling in reverse, had been caught in the closing doors of the lock, as firmly as if the ship had been grasped by giant pliers. The engines strained and bellowed, and smoke started pouring up from the engine room as the screws fought to propel the vessel but met the solid resistance of the doors' vise grip.

The impact had floored the soldiers on the foredeck as well, and Paine knew he would never get a better chance than this one. He sprung to his feet, firing as he rose, and put two big slugs into the head of the soldier nearest the wheelhouse. Paine's gun jerked a degree to the left and fired: a second commando went down in a tangle of arms and legs, sprawling on the lumber, and lying still as death.

A burp of automatic-weapons fire demolished a part of the wheel to Paine's right. A soldier was crouched next to the lumber, firing from a narrow slice of deck between the cargo and the taffrails. Paine's big weapon came around and he fired three times, twice splintering part of the finished wood, but the third hit flesh. The soldier grunted and slipped over the side into the roiling water. Bullets peppered the wheelhouse, and Paine dropped to the deck. Blood had trailed down one side of his face and had soaked the collar and shoulder of his rough-spun jacket.

The return fire from the Vopos told him that they were spooked, firing blind, hoping that they would get lucky. All he had to do was stay down and wait for his moment—he prayed that the gunfire would let up for a second or two.

It was then that Halbach struck. The young man whipped a knife out of a sheath tied to his ankle and dove for Paine, knocking the gun from his hands. Halbach was strong, a lot stronger than he looked. He wrestled Paine back from the gun, but the American was able to get a lock grip on the hand that held the knife, keeping it clear. His left hand formed itself into an iron-hard fist and slammed into Halbach's belly. The punch, as hard as Paine could muster, didn't seem to have much effect: his fist met hard, unyielding muscle, and the young man hardly grunted as the blow crashed into him.

Halbach's left hand grasped Paine's, immobilizing it, preventing him from doing further damage. Then the German bore down, pushing back against Paine, forcing his knife hand inexorably toward Paine's throat.

Wilson, curled in a ball in a corner of the wheelhouse, whimpered as the waves of bullets poured through the shattered glass. All he had to do was get Paine's gun—he could have reached out and grabbed it—and finish Halbach off, but with every rip of bullets, the young scientist cinched himself a little tighter. Great, thought Paine; next thing you know, he'll do some yoga and fall asleep.

There was only one way to get rid of Halbach, Paine decided, and that was to have his own side get rid of him. Summoning up every ounce of strength he possessed, Paine flexed his arms and legs, throwing the German up and off of him and into the murderous hail of fire that still crashed through the window. A half dozen shots slammed into Halbach's body, tearing into his back in the second he was exposed to the fire. He tumbled to the floor of the wheelhouse, a messy tatter of blood, flesh, and clothing.

For a second the firing stopped, and Paine wasted no time getting to his feet. He snatched up the gun and fired at another soldier who was trying to climb on the wheelhouse roof, firing through the small skylight. Bullets still rained down on the ship, but they came from the top of the lock, and firing was inaccurate and wild.

Time to go, thought Paine. He grabbed Wilson by the scruff of the neck and threw him out onto the fantail of the ship. The doors were still straining like giant jaws against the wooden sides of the barge, and the timbers were beginning to buckle and snap. But the ship had wedged the doors open, enough daylight for them to dive through and into the cold, oily waters of the river.

"When you hit the water, swim like hell!" he ordered Wilson, and without waiting for a reply, shoved the young man toward the water. Before Paine followed him, he made sure that Wilson came up from the wake; he saw him flailing through the water in the general direction of escape. That was good enough. Paine dove into the water, broke clean to the surface, and started swimming. As he came up for air, he saw Wilson's head bobbing ahead of him; that was something to be thankful for. The backwash of the still-straining engines worked in their favor, shooting them through the water as if they were Malibu body surfers.

When Paine estimated that they were three quarters of a mile from the lock, he caught up with Wilson and dragged him into the shallows by the riverbank. The industrial areas that lined the waterfront were dotted with piers and rotting docks and tall, towering piles of scrap metal in rusting storeyards. Paine knew they had to get out of the water and get warm soon or they would be too weak for the next part of the journey. The mist was still down, and while he could hear heavy activity on the river— shouts and the occasional shot—he sensed that they were pretty safe in the industrial crust that lined the river.

Paine left Wilson floating in the shallows while he staggered ashore, scouting the territory a hundred yards inland. There was half an acre of rusting steel drums, some of them oozing some kind of revolting, high-smelling liquid into the stained earth: some of the East's highly organized system of toxic-waste disposal, he imagined. Beyond the field of rusting drums was a squat corrugated iron shed. It was the only shelter Paine could see, so it would have to do.

He returned to the riverbank and pulled Wilson from the water. The young man didn't look good. He had probably swallowed half of the polluted river in the course of his swim. He gagged as he was dragged from the water and stopped twice as they threaded their way through the drums to puke some of the stinking water he had swallowed. He started to groan, but Paine slapped an oily hand over his mouth; he held a finger to his lips: they had to be absolutely silent if they were to survive.

Paine broke open the door of the shed, and both men collapsed on the concrete floor. In those moments after action like that, Paine could feel the fatigue spreading through him. But he fought the desire for sleep; he had to stay alert.

Wilson seemed to understand that too. He heaved himself up and over to a corner, where he vomited up the last of the river water, and then, Paine thought, the young man did something very much out of character: he tried to kill him.

7

Suddenly it all came clear: the ability to sleep under tight circumstances, the flawless German—Wilson was an agent, one of theirs. The rest—the nervousness, the gawkiness, even the feigned cowardice on the barge—had been an act, and a damn good one. Under fire, Wilson, or whatever his real name was, could keep in character, remain behind his cover—no mean feat, hard to do at the best of times, even harder to do when someone was shooting at you.

The all-thumbs act was gone for good, that was for sure. Wilson, like a good actor, had shed his science-nerd persona and assumed his real character. He was a tall man, thin but wiry, and suddenly, to Paine, he looked almost invincible. But there was one thing Paine had on his side: experience. In the moment before the fight began, while Paine had been concentrating on the enemy around him, hardly expecting an attack from Wilson's quarter, Wilson should have struck and struck hard. Paine would have been a sitting duck. But Wilson had blown it, hesitating long enough for Paine to look up, and then confirming his turncoat status with a nice, high karate scream, just the way they taught you in close-combat training. In most cases a yell like that scared the bejesus out of you; in this case it gave Paine an essential split second to get ready.

He was on his feet before Wilson could land the first blow. What would have been a devastating chop to his shoulder just grazed Paine's forearm, setting it tingling like he had slept on it, but hardly a knockout blow. For his trouble, Wilson received a hard, sharp spear kick to the chest, throwing him back against the thin walls. He was winded, but professional enough to have his guard up when Paine moved in, snapping him back with a right, which opened up the scabbed cuts on Paine's cheek. Wilson's hard fist came away bloody, and the sight of the gore seemed to stimulate him. He attacked again, the kick forgotten, throwing all of his power behind his fists.

They were blows Paine could tell were powerful enough to fell an oak, but he parried them and ducked under a wide roundhouse right, slamming two hard fists into Wilson's midsection. The effect was not unlike the punches he had landed on Halbach—he felt as if his knuckles had been broken. Whoever trained these goddamn kids was good.

I have got to stop doing that, he reminded himself.

Wilson's legs had scissored under Paine, and he went down hard on the concrete floor. The sole of Wilson's heavy bargeman's boot filled his vision as he tried to stomp down on Paine's face the way you'd crush a bug underfoot. Paine's bruised hands shot up and grabbed the boot and he turned it, like a steering wheel in a skid. He could almost hear the snap of muscles and tendons in the ankle, and Wilson's eyes grew wide with pain.

"Jesus Ker-ist!"

That told Paine something: that Wilson was either a deep sleeper, an American agent who worked for the East but was so assimilated that he even expressed pain in English, or that he really was an American. The first order of business, though, was to put the man out of commission; he'd find out who he was later.

The searing pain in Wilson's leg would have stopped an agent twice as dedicated. He retreated, unthinkingly putting weight down on his injured ankle, screaming again, and then trying to hop away from Paine, who was on his feet again.

John Paine had had a long day, a long week, in fact. Suddenly he thought back to the incident in the park in Rome, the sleazy Club Paradiso, Cannon's sneer, the breakdown of Coyote 1, the scene on the boat, the double—or was it triple?—cross. Enough with finesse, he thought, no more Langley rules. Paine wanted some peace and quiet so he could think his way out of this jam, get back to the West, and find out just what in hell was going on.

He picked up a handy piece of wood, about the size of an American two-by-four, and brained Wilson, whanging the club down on the back of the man's head as he comically tried to hop toward the door.

"Uh," said Wilson eloquently, and he toppled to the floor, smacking his forehead on the concrete. Paine hoped he had concussed himself.

He sat for a moment getting his breath back and calming his racing heart, then he searched Wilson, finding nothing that gave a clue to his real identity. That didn't surprise him.

Paine thought for a minute or two, then quickly unlaced Wilson's boots and tugged down his pants. Then he started on his shirt and underwear. In a matter of minutes, Wilson was naked on the cold floor. Paine tore up his shirt and bound his hands as tightly as he could, then balled the rest of the clothes up in a bundle and headed for the door of the shed.

Robbing a man of his clothes, a psychological warfare specialist had explained to him once, leaves him almost helpless. Rare is the man who will be able to stand the humiliation of walking naked into the streets to look for help or refuge; true, it had been done, but there was some visceral fear that had to be overcome in order to accomplish it. Paine had a feeling that Wilson wasn't that courageous.

Paine himself didn't look exactly inconspicuous. His cheek was bleeding, his clothes were filthy and wet, his hair was dirty and matted, and his sodden boots squished with every step. He tossed Wilson's clothes into an open drum of noxious chemicals, half expecting to see them fizzle up and melt in the brew, but was satisfied when they merely sunk to the bottom of the liquid. A very brave man—braver than Paine— would think twice about rooting around in that muck in search of his clothes: he'd probably pull his arm out to discover that he was an amputee. He doubted that a concussed, naked Wilson would try it, hopping around on one good leg.

Paine made his way cautiously through the dump and beyond the rusting factory that faced it. He found a metal door, secured only with old wire, and bust it open as quietly as he could manage. The sound seemed to boom through the factory, and Paine was sure that every Vopo within a hundred miles could hear it. Beyond the door was a parking lot and a tall gate, which sagged open; beyond that, a street. Paine took a deep breath and walked as nonchalantly as he could through the gate and into the real world and smack into a man walking a dog. He was an elderly man, about the age of the skipper on the barge, and dressed like a worker, but he had a creased, kindly face and looked at Paine in alarm. The dog immediately started sniffing a whole raft of interesting smells on Paine's trousers.

"Are you all right?" asked the man.

Paine prayed his German would hold. "*Ja*," he said, "I had a fall." He nodded toward the factory. "In there."

"What were you doing in there?"

Paine did his best to smile. "Even in an abandoned factory there's always something to steal."

Paine had hoped that the man would smile conspiratorially, but he didn't. He frowned. "That's none of my business."

"You're right."

"But you better watch out, my friend; the police are all over the place. I think someone tried to go over."

"Damn! Just my luck. Where are they?"

"All about. I saw a patrol down there." He pointed toward the way he had come. "I'm on my way, thank you very much. I didn't see you."

"Thanks," said Paine.

"You should be more careful."

"Don't worry. I will in future."

The man yanked his dog away from Paine's cuffs and hurried away. Paine congratulated himself on his German and walked in the opposite direction. He passed a couple of other men, who looked at his disheveled clothes with some curiosity but said nothing. Paine was in a factory district, which counted in his favor, and besides, the East Berliners weren't exactly world-famous for being fashion plates. Nonetheless, he was pleased and relieved when he found the object of his search: a phone booth.

While the East Berliner's physical access to the West is heavily curtailed, the two cities share a telephone system that allows anyone with fifty pfennigs in his pocket to call into the West; phone traffic between the two parts of the city is so heavy that not even the East German secret police could monitor all the calls. The CIA emergency number in West Berlin was as cold as such a number could be, and Paine was reasonably sure that his call was not listened in on, although, nonetheless, he knew the duty officer scrambled the transmission just to be on the safe side.

Paine didn't recognize the voice that answered, but he didn't expect to—the Berlin bureau was restaffed so frequently that the turnover in personnel was hard to keep track of. For every old soldier like Sam Grove who stayed year after year, there were a dozen understaffers who were shipped in and out each year. It kept the East and the KGB busy trying to identify operatives, soaking up time that could be used for more productive espionage.

The procedure for bringing a downed agent out of the Eastern side of the wall was pretty standard. Paine was given an address and a time and told that one of the inviolable army patrols would pick him up within two hours. If he couldn't make that rendezvous, there was a fallback position, which Paine, now feeling the effects of combat, wearing tension, and plain old fatigue, hoped he wouldn't have to use.

"There's just one problem," said Paine.

"Which is?"

"There are two of us. And the other one's a hostile."

There was a sigh on the other end of the line. "Hostile? You've captured one of theirs?"

"It's a long story."

"I'll bet it is." Taking an East German national, or a Russian or whatever the hell Wilson was, out of the East zone was a tricky proposition. If the East chose to make a stink about it, a public stink, they would claim that one of their countrymen had been kidnapped—which he had—secure in the knowledge that the U.S. consul in West Germany or the Embassy in Bonn could not reveal the true story.

If the East kept quiet, things could be just as bad. It was an open invitation for them to grab an American agent on his own home turf, tit for tat.

"I better check with the brass," said the duty officer.

"Well, hurry up."

"Relax. This line is secure."

Well, I'm not, thought Paine. He waited a minute or two before the voice came back on the line.

"Your instructions are to bring him out."

"Fine," Paine said, and hung up, wondering

how he was going to get a disabled and hostile Wilson across the city to the safe house pickup point.

Cautiously he retraced his steps to the factory. The streets seemed quiet now, with no one conspicuously loitering on a street corner reading a newspaper; neither was there much traffic. The factory seemed as deserted as Paine had left it, and all was calm inside the shed. Maybe he'll come quietly, Paine thought.

Wilson was quiet, but he wasn't going anywhere. He was still naked, but he had come to at some point and had managed to crawl a few feet toward the door. There, he had killed himself in the time-honored agent's manner: a tooth that had been hollowed and refilled with some kind of poison. It wasn't cyanide anymore—that had gone out with the Cold War—but whatever it had been was extremely effective: Wilson was stone cold dead.

In a second, Paine reconstructed the last events of Wilson's life. He had come to and had decided that trussed and naked though he was, his training told him he had to escape. He had made it as far as the door when reality kicked in: he wouldn't get free and he had to assume that Paine was coming back for him; he further assumed that Wilson would reveal who he was working for. It was, it seemed, quite literally a fate worse than death. Wilson had killed himself, taking his secrets with him.

Paine slumped against the door of the shed

and shook his head. Although he was exhausted, he felt himself consumed by curiosity: who the hell was Wilson really, and what the hell was going on? Well, if he couldn't take Wilson with him, then he could at least try and find out who the hell he was.

He rolled the dead man's right hand in a patch of oil on the cement floor and then pressed it hard against an old piece of newspaper he found in the corner of the shed. He held the paper up to the light and looked at the impression of the corpse's fingerprints. He was not pleased with his handiwork and doubted that anyone could take a clear reading from the impression. Paine folded the paper carefully and put it in his pocket, then he went outside searching among the rubble till he found what he needed: a heavy shard of glass from one of the smashed windows. He returned to the shed, not looking forward to the next part.

Doing violence to a man who had attacked him came easily to Paine; mutilating a corpse was another matter entirely. He took a deep breath and grabbed the thumb on the right hand of the body, bending it backward quickly until the bone snapped at the second joint. The thumb wobbled a bit in its socket, like a drumstick on a well-cooked Thanksgiving turkey. Paine stretched the skin taut and sliced into the joint with the piece of glass, cutting a ragged, bloody gash in the meat of the thumb. He forced the glass into the joint and tried to lever the finger out of the socket, but he put too much pressure on the bone, and the glass snapped.

"Shit!" The hand fell back, landing on Wilson's chest, throwing a stain of blood up to his muscular neck. Paine rubbed his eyes and cursed silently, hating Wilson and hating what he had to do. He steeled himself again and took a firm grip on the hand, jamming the glass into the cut again and working it back and forth until the point of his makeshift blade emerged on the other side of Wilson's mangled hand. The thumb hung now by a few shreds of skin and a piece of obstinate gristle, and it took Paine another few minutes to saw through. Finally, with a sickening parting of skin and bone, the digit came free and Paine dropped it immediately on the cold floor.

"The things I do for Old Glory," he said aloud. He forced himself to pick up the finger and wrapped it in a piece of filthy rag. He jammed it into his jacket pocket and tried to forget it was there, hoping that the severed thumb had done all the bleeding it was going to do.

Paine was glad to leave the corpse and the shed behind him, even if it meant going out into the unwelcoming world of East Berlin. At least now he was moving, alone, and heading toward rescue. A light rain had started to fall, and Paine figured that worked in his favor, clearing the streets of most pedestrians; those who remained had their umbrellas up or their heads down, scurrying along the wet pavements toward shelter. Perhaps, just perhaps, they wouldn't pay any attention to him. The passersby worried him just as much as the police; policemen, he could identify, but pedestrians were a closed book. They might be anxious to avoid trouble like the old man walking the dog, or they might wish to score some brownie points with the Vopos by reporting a suspicious-looking stranger. East Germans were notorious informers, and Paine knew he would have a fair bit of explaining to do if he was stopped by a patrol. He could think of no plausible reason for having a human thumb in his pocket. He doubted if anyone could.

8

The residents of Neuenhagen on the eastern edge of the city had long since grown accustomed to seeing the patrols of the Western powers wandering through their dirty streets. Under the Four Powers agreement, every army of the victorious Allies had the right to inspect the other's real estate whenever they wanted. Usually this was a strictly proforma procedure—both sides would have been content to let the patrols lapse, but didn't for fear that the other side would continue them if they made a unilateral announcement. There had been wrangling between East and West Germany for years on the subject, but nothing had been achieved, so the patrols continued.

True, once in a while a patrol had a specific intelligence goal, and sometimes things got messy. A few years ago an American Army major had been shot and killed by the Vopos. They claimed that he had strayed too close to a sensitive military installation, and despite the stern exchange of notes between the American government and the GDR, nothing had come of it—it was assumed that the DIA major had been playing fast and loose with the rules and had been caught. That was the way the game was played.

So Paine knew there was a measure of danger involved in what he was about to do, no matter the bored tone of the controller at the other end of the CIA emergency line. He waited as patiently as he could for the army patrol to roll through the workers' housing precinct in Neuenhagen, hoping that the rain, which had intensified, would make the Easterners that little bit sloppy. The morning's bust-up in the canal lock probably had all the intelligence and security services out in force, and they would be watching the patrol carefully. That was to be expected but was not insurmountable—once Paine had met up with his rescuers, then he was safe: again, under the Four Powers agreement, a patrol could not be stopped and searched. The French, British, and Americans hated that proviso when the Russians tried something on their side of the wall, but they didn't mind it a bit when they were after something in hostile territory.

Paine was surprised to see not an American or even a British patrol that afternoon in Neuenhagen, but a French one. Two three-ton Citroen trucks and a Renault staff car came cruising along, stopping dead in the middle of the street where a group of children were playing soccer. Three hundred yards behind the French procession was the Eastern shadow, a Borgward jeep containing three soldiers and an officer.

A French captain emerged from the staff car and walked smartly back toward the jeep as if on a very important mission. Hanging off the back of one of the trucks was a French soldier, the rest of the squad keeping dry under canvas.

Paine stepped off the curb and into the melee of the soccer game. He shoved aside one of the kids, who was dribbling the ball toward the opposing goal, and kicked the ball hard out of bounds.

The kids yelped in anger and chased after the black and white ball, yelling hoarse curses at the big bully who had interrupted their game. Paine darted under one of the trucks and felt four hands reach down through a hatch in the bed and pull him up. There were six soldiers sitting there, a couple puffing on Gauloises, their FN rifles neatly stacked.

"*Op la,*" said one as he heaved Paine into the truck.

"*Merci,*" said Paine. His French was no better than his German, and knowing how touchy the French were about foreigners speaking their language incorrectly, he decided to keep his words to a minimum.

Another soldier slung a bundle of clothes at

105

him and told him, in French, to put them on. It was the uniform of a corporal in one of the chasseur regiments, and after Paine had dressed himself in the summer-weight tunic and pants, one of the soldiers buttoned on his rank badges and flashes. He settled on the bench next to one of the soldiers, accepted a Gauloise, and tried to look as bored as the rest of the soldiers.

The French officer from the staff car finished his altercation with his East German opposite number, returned to his automobile, and gave the order for advance. Half an hour later, the little convoy rolled into the French sector of West Berlin.

It was obvious that Charlie Sullivan and Sam Grove were not happy. Grove sat slumped behind his high-tech desk, his shoulders sagging and his face sunk in a jowly frown. Sullivan was antsy, walking from one end of the room to the other until Grove growled at him.

"For Christ's sake, Charlie, would you sit down? That pacing is driving me crazy."

Sullivan sat, but one leg jiggled up and down as if he was ready to bound out of his seat at the slightest provocation. Paine sat in front of Sam Grove's desk. He had showered and changed and had something to eat. He was still bone-tired. Wilson's thumb, wrapped in a hand towel stolen from his hotel, was nestled in his jacket pocket.

"Oh, Johnny, Johnny, Johnny," said Grove. "What a fucking mess."

"You can say that again," echoed Sullivan. It struck Paine that that was one of the few times he had ever heard Sullivan agree with his chief.

"I was set up."

"Oh bullshit!"

Paine glanced at Sullivan with contempt.

"It couldn't have been easier, Paine. You were sent over there on a simple mission and you screwed it up."

"Shall I tell you again? Should I start from the top and tell you how Hartmann turned out to be an officer in the Vopos? How Halbach and Wilson tried to kill me? You think I make things like that up?"

Sullivan shook his head shortly. "I just think you could have come out of it a little better."

"Oh Christ," said Paine.

Sam Grove spoke. "The point is, Johnny, that you're hot here, and you're hot in Rome. What we've decided is that you have to take a little leave, calm down, take it easy."

"Hold it. Isn't anyone besides me interested in what happened over there? This isn't just a case of something not working out, this was a goddamn trap. Someone was gunning for me—"

"For you!" snorted Sullivan derisively. "What the hell do they care about you? What the hell would they want you for?" There was something in Sullivan's voice that suggested he wished that whatever the East's motives, they had succeeded in getting Paine.

"Maybe not me personally, but they wanted to spring a trap. They wanted—"

"They probably wanted Wilson to work on their neo-bio-whatever the hell they are. They got plenty of goons over there, Paine; what the hell do they need one of ours for?"

Paine felt a hot pulse of anger pass through him. That was all Sullivan thought he was: a goon, a hit man, a glorified gangster.

"They already owned Wilson," Paine shot back. "He was one of them. He tried to kill me. Explain that."

"Maybe you should explain why it was that he ended up dead. You killed him."

"I didn't," said Paine.

"We only have your word for that."

"Sullivan—" Paine had risen from his seat.

"Oh yeah, big tough John Paine," Sullivan taunted. "Gonna off me now?"

"Shuttup," ordered Grove. "Charlie, you are out of line. Johnny, you are close to being out of line. So both of you shuttup. Got it?"

They both shut up.

"Okay. As of today, Johnny, you're on leave. Also as of today, an investigation into this whole mess begins."

"Start with Wilson," said Paine. "Find out who he is."

"Was," corrected Sullivan. "He was a serving

officer of the CIA technical services. That's who he was, dammit."

"Who tried to kill a serving member of the CIA operational service," said Paine. "There's something about him that you haven't discovered, Sullivan. He was working for the other side. Last time I checked, that was against our rules."

"We'll do a complete background. Charlie, get cracking."

"Good," said Paine. "Start with this." He pulled the towel out of his pocket. "Here, Sullivan." He tossed it across the room and Sullivan caught it. He folded back the towel and stared for a moment at the bloody finger.

"Jesus Christ!" He stared hard at Paine. "Torture give you your kicks now?"

"What the hell is it?" demanded Grove.

"It's a thumb," explained Paine. "Wilson's thumb. I couldn't get a good impression of his fingerprints."

"So you cut off his thumb? Why not his whole goddam hand?".

"I didn't have a sharp knife, Mr. Sullivan. Next time..."

"Wait," said Grove. "Johnny, let me get this straight. You cut off Wilson's thumb?"

"His right one. He was dead already."

"Well, thank heaven for small mercies," said Sullivan.

"I didn't want to do it. I didn't enjoy it. It's

not the kind of thing I go in for. But you're going to have to begin ID somewhere."

"Under the circumstances," said Grove, "I'd say it was necessary. Forget you had to do it."

Paine had found over the years that he wasn't very good at forgetting things. He shifted uneasily in the chair. "So now what? What do we do next?"

Grove and Sullivan exchanged glances. "I don't think 'we' have to do anything."

"So I'm out," said Paine flatly.

"In a nutshell."

"Sorry, Johnny. Take your leave and leave this to us."

Paine got to his feet. "Nobody wants my debrief?"

"I think we know enough," said Sullivan.

"Well, I'm glad you do, because I don't. I have no idea what's going on."

"That's another thing, Johnny," said Grove quietly. "I don't want you sneaking around, using your own time to look into things. We've got enough trouble as it is."

"Sam, I wouldn't know where to begin."

"Good. Scram."

Paine spent the night in Berlin, and early the next morning he was flown by helicopter to Hannover, the largest German city near Berlin. At the airport he was met by the local American consul, a rosy-cheeked young man deeply impressed with himself at having been chosen for CIA business.

He handed over Paine's new papers and ten thousand dollars in traveler's checks with the solemnity of a religious ceremony. It gave the young consul a little thrill to actually meet a spy in person—his first—and it was all he could do to prevent himself from trying to get Paine to tell him what he had done on the other side of the wall. It was like something out of a John Le Carre novel.

"And these are the keys to your car," he said, sliding a set of keys across the table of the airport coffee shop. Paine was puzzled by the young man—it was as if he were passing secrets to the other side. The consul kept on glancing around as if expecting a KGB hit squad to appear at any moment.

"Thank you."

"I'm afraid it's nothing fancy. Just an Opel."

"That'll do nicely."

"Good. Is there anything else?"

"Nope," said Paine. "Thanks for all your trouble."

The consul flushed. "No trouble."

The first thing Paine did was change all of the money into deutsch marks, receiving a thick wad of bills for his traveler's checks. If he wandered around Europe cashing the checks, he'd leave a paper trail that a blind man could follow. He intended to follow Grove's orders and leave the investigation to the Berlin bureau, but he hated the idea of leaving such an obvious trail. It was just his training and he couldn't fight it.

The consul was right, the Opel was nothing fancy, but that was just fine with him. Fancy cars attracted attention, and it always amused him when movie secret agents, à la James Bond, drove some high-priced, high-powered machine. Most of the company cars that Paine had used over the years had been down-at-the-heel automobiles that no one ever even saw, let alone remembered. As cars went, the Opel was better than most. It was a standard rental model and was clean and well serviced. It didn't have much pickup, but Paine didn't figure to be going anywhere in a hurry.

In the airport parking lot he examined his new identity. He was James Deveraux—he grimaced slightly when he read the name; it was a noticeable name—from Cleveland. He didn't like the place of birth much either: he had never been to Cleveland. He reminded himself, though, that many Americans didn't live where they had been born. Paine relocated himself in New York, a city he knew well.

He put the car in gear and drove out of Hannover, heading south. No one, not even Paine, was sure of where he was going.

Sam Grove had been in his office for about a minute that morning when Charlie Sullivan came in carrying a folder and wearing a look of unmistakable triumph. Grove knew immediately that he was in for a bad time, the kind of bad time that only Charlie Sullivan was capable of inflicting. It was no secret that Sullivan thought Grove over the hill and that the Berlin chair would be better filled by one Charles Sullivan. Any chance he got to embarrass his superior, he seized with relish.

He put down the folder, placing it squarely in the middle of Grove's desk, the way a house cat drops a rat at the feet of its master. Grove looked up unhappily.

"Why don't you just tell me, Charlie?"

"Guess who Wilson was?"

"Amelia Earhart?"

"Ha ha. No, really."

"Tell me, Charlie."

"He was Allen H. Wilson. Born Cos Cob, Connecticut, June 12, 1950. Educated at Caltech..."

"Et cetera. Get on with it."

"He was exactly who he said he was. Everything checks out. Even the thumb. He was one of us, Sam."

"Shit."

"You're damn right, shit. Paine killed a serving member of the Central Intelligence Agency."

"Christ, what the hell do you think happened over there?"

"It's obvious..."

"To you, maybe. Explain."

"Paine's gone over. He was supposed to prevent Halbach from coming over; Wilson found out about it and he tried to stop him. End of

Wilson. Paine gets out—mighty easily—and back into the welcoming arms of the CIA. It's obvious, Sam; Paine's a double."

"No he isn't."

Sullivan sat down and smiled. "Why don't we run it by Langley and see what they say." Sullivan was pleased. This had to mean the end of Sam Grove—and he'd take a dangerous man like John Paine with him. A good day's work—and the working day wasn't five minutes old.

9

The director of the European desk of the Central Intelligence Agency in Langley, Virginia, was a methodical, careful man named Arthur Endicott. He had a fine career behind him, having served as station chief in both London and Paris, as well as Washington liaison for the Nato intelligence network. His position on the European desk would be his last. He was approaching retirement and he was happy about that. Endicott liked his job, but he was a realist; the great days of European intelligence were gone. The glory days of the Great Game played out in picture book villages of West Germany were the stuff that old guys like Endicott reminisced about. Now he ran things well and soberly, with a minimum of fuss. The European section meeting that Wednesday morning was troubling, deeply troubling.

There were three other men in his office sipping coffee and looking grave. There was

Calder, head of the German section, Weinberg, Endicott's deputy chief, and Kevin Cunningham, invited in because he knew Paine better than anyone.

"It's a question of who to believe," said Calder, pushing his heavy horn-rimmed glasses back up his shiny nose. "Think what you want about John Paine, he's never shown the slightest tendency, never given a hint that he might be a double."

Cunningham shifted as best he could in his wheelchair. John Paine never gave anything away, not unless he wanted to. He could have been working for half the intelligence services in the world and you wouldn't know about it. A desk man like Calder would never understand that a field agent like Paine made a professional card player look gregarious and outgoing.

"Still," said Endicott, "Sullivan is sure..."

"Sullivan, as we all know, has his reasons for making Sam Grove look bad," added Weinberg. He was a young man, generally considered too young to take over Endicott's job when he retired—still, Cunningham was sure he would get it when the time came. Weinberg was a master of office politics and he was hungry for power.

Endicott shrugged. "We lost Wilson. Halbach may or may not have been a double. Overall, I'd say that it was a mess. The only person who walked out was Paine. How do you figure that?"

Cunningham finally spoke. "Because he's good enough to get out of a tight situation. John will always keep his head, and that's how you survive."

"That and a lot of luck," said Calder as if he knew all about it.

"That too."

"If Paine is solid, then what about Wilson?"

All three men shrugged. No one had known Wilson; it was impossible to know every one of the twenty thousand or so CIA employees. For the controllers the tech side was terra incognita.

Cunningham frowned. He didn't like the "*if* Paine is solid . . ."

"Kevin," said Endicott, "you don't look happy."

"It's hard to be. As you all know, John Paine is a close friend of mine and I hate to hear his loyalty questioned. If things happened the way he said they did, then that's good enough for me."

"Perhaps you're being blinded by your friendship," said Weinberg.

Cunningham shook his head. "No. It's because we're friends that I know he's telling the truth."

Weinberg just shrugged.

"On the strength of Paine's distinguished record," said Endicott, "I'm inclined to believe his version of events."

"But what about Wilson?" insisted Calder.

"He's being vacuumed thoroughly. The backcheck that Sullivan ordered was not as deep as it could have been. We're taking Wilson apart to see if there was anything that could suggest that he was a . . ." It was as if Weinberg couldn't bring himself to say the dreaded word: sleeper, an agent buried so deep in the fabric, not just of the CIA but of the United States, that he was all but undetectable.

"Alec," said Endicott, turning to Calder, "you okayed the Halbach operation. How the hell did you get hold of it?"

"It was straightforward. Halbach had been passing some information through Sentry—" Calder glanced at Cunningham. "I'm sorry, Kevin; are you cleared on Sentry?"

Cunningham nodded.

Sentry was a well-placed spy in the Ministry of Industry in East Berlin. He had been reporting for the CIA for years, apparently undetected.

"Sentry passed on that Halbach wanted to come over. I ran it by the technical people and Rafferty, and it looked good. Wilson had to go in to meet some other German scientist named Hartmann. You know as well as I that the tech side doesn't make a lot of sense if you have anything less than a Ph.D. But they wanted him, and I set it up with Grove and Sullivan. It was that simple."

"Except it wasn't," observed Weinberg.

"No," agreed Calder. "It wasn't."

"So," said Endicott. "Does anyone have any ideas about what to do next?"

"I think we should see what Sentry has to say," said Weinberg.

"Alec, that's your baby."

Calder nodded. "And when we know more about Wilson, then we should have a clearer idea of just what the hell went on over there."

"And Paine?" Endicott turned to Weinberg. "What do you think? Should we bring him back here and talk him through?"

Cunningham frowned again. Talking through was a very nice way of saying they wanted to give Paine the third degree, complete with bright lights and disorienting time frames and lack of sleep—everything but drugs and thumbscrews. "If you do that," said Cunningham, "then you'll lose him. I'll tell you now: he won't change his story, and when the talk-through is over, he'll walk out the front door of this place and you'll never see him again. John's greatest . . . flaw, I guess, is his pride. He'd take pride in breaking the talkers, but he'd never let himself get in that position again. You talk through with him and that's the last you'll see of him."

Weinberg looked a little angry. "Every member of this service knows that there is a chance this could happen to them at some point in their career. Paine can't be treated any different. He knows the rules."

"A full-scale interrogation like that is, I believe, reserved for serving members who come under suspicion of dealing with the other side.

As I see it, Paine was involved in an operation that went sour. He used his training and his skills and got himself out of it, and it would seem to me that he performed just as the Agency would have wanted him to. He left no mess . . ."

"He killed Wilson," observed Calder.

"Wilson killed Wilson."

"Either way. A serving member of this Agency was killed."

"But one escaped. Assuming Wilson wasn't a double, that he was one of us, Paine should be thanked for getting out; they would have a field agent and a tech staff member. Instead, they look ridiculous. I wouldn't be surprised if there are some heads rolling around Karl Marx Strasse."

Calder shook his head. "You can hardly call this a triumph, Kevin."

"No, but the damage was controlled."

"And a man is dead. One of ours," said Weinberg.

"We don't know that." Endicott shuffled some papers on his desk. "This is what I propose," he said without looking up. "I think that we should give Paine his lead. Keep him in Europe, but we'll have to keep an eye on him. He's no fool, of course, he's going to be expecting something like that, but we'll have to do our best. Alec, you see what Sentry has to say. And I"—he sighed—"will go talk to the DCI."

Endicott and Calder left the room first, but Weinberg lingered behind offering to help Cunningham maneuver his wheelchair through the door and down the hall. It was precisely the type of gesture Cunningham hated.

"I can handle it," he said. And he could—he had been in the damn thing close to twenty years. His massive arm swung the chair around and pointed it at the door, which was comfortably wide. All federal buildings—even the CIA—had to be accessible for the handicapped (another term Cunningham hated). Before he could wheel himself out—as a wheelchair marathoner, Cunningham disdained motorized chairs—Weinberg stopped him.

"Kevin..."

Cunningham wheeled around. "Yes, Tom?" Weinberg was rarely known as anything other than Weinberg.

"If Paine should get in touch with you..." Weinberg was hoping that Cunningham would just pick up on his meaning, rather than force him to say something he didn't want to say.

Cunningham refused to play ball. "What about it, Tom?"

"Well, I think, under the circumstances, it would be wise for you to report anything he has to say."

"Fine. I'll tell him that."

Weinberg licked his lips nervously. "That's not what I had in mind exactly, Kevin."

"And what did you have in mind exactly, Tom?"

"I'd prefer that you didn't let on that you were

reporting your conversations. That's assuming, of course, that he ever gets in touch with you."

"Oh. I get it. You want me to spy on a friend of mine. Betray his confidences, that kind of thing, right?"

"Kevin, under the circumstances . . . I mean to say, this is something of great importance to the Agency. We have to be sure of Paine." Weinberg forestalled the response he knew Cunningham was bound to make. "And we can't just take your word for it." The tone of Weinberg's voice changed; he spoke almost as if issuing an order. "If you hear from him, I want you to tell me what he says. Okay?"

Cunningham nodded. "Sure thing, Tom."

"Good."

Both men knew Cunningham was lying.

10

Slowly Paine drifted south, feeling the call of
the Mediterranean pulling him down along the
eastern edge of the Federal Republic of West
Germany. He was in no hurry, and kept his
speedometer needle firmly on one hundred kilometers an hour, giving the no-limit lane a wide
berth. Big Mercedes and BMWs swept by him
as if he were standing still, silvery cars with
anxious men at the wheels, rich men hurrying
to Göttingen or Kassel or the gray sprawl of
Frankfurt to sell, to close a deal, to get richer,
to avoid ruin.

Sometimes, when a 500SEL had zoomed past,
Paine found himself envying the man behind
the wheel. How easy it must be, he thought, to
worry about nothing but money; in business
there was deceit and betrayal, but never death
and torture. And the rewards were concrete:
something as simple as money; you could count
it, spend it, throw it away. It was yours to do
what you wanted.

The rewards that Paine could expect—the satisfaction of having done a good job, the simple pleasure of beating a rival, the sense of doing one's duty—were intangible and anonymous. Few people would know about them, but that didn't bother him so much; a famous agent was a dead agent, or, worse, useless.

It took him three days to drive to the Bavarian border, through countryside with names redolent of the Second World War, the Last Good War, his father used to call it, as well as names to become famous in the war yet to come. There was Fulda, the home of the Fulda Gap, a natural door into Germany exploited by the Russians in the second war and which still gave nightmares to the men in NATO charged with winning the third.

Then there was Nuremberg. He arrived in bright sunshine, but the city seemed still cast in the shadows of the War Crimes Commission, as if the blame of the entire country had been permanently affixed to this one town. Next came Munich, so cute it seemed not to be real; Hitler's favorite town.

In the few days that had passed since he had left the earnest young consul at the airport in Hannover, Paine had spoken little. A few words to waiters, hotel clerks, gas station attendants. He had some good—some would say memorable—meals in small restaurants in small towns. He had fought a losing battle with his training by almost unconsciously registering the units and number of vehicles of the American Army convoys that had passed him on the autobahn. He wondered about the satellites hovering high above the earth watching these convoys, the millions of dollars spent on surveillance that could have been accomplished by any reasonably talented amateur driving leisurely from the Baltic to the Alps. He shrugged. Ah well, it was not his worry.

As he drove, he thought, trying to order the events of the recent past, trying to make sense of them, looking for a pattern that might tie them all together. The kid in the park in Rome. He wasn't supposed to have backup. Was that significant or had Paine's information been a little off? It made sense to send someone along to make sure the kid did his job—he was an amateur, and there was no telling how badly he could screw things up. If Paine had been in control of the operation, he would have made sure that the kid had a helping hand, just in case.

But the kid was trying to kill Paine just about the time Coyote 1 was being rounded up. Was that just a coincidence? If Paine had been killed, he would never have known about the destruction of an operation he himself had created.

The debacle in Berlin. Who was that aimed at? The Agency in general or Paine in particular? All the facts said the Agency: Slipping Wilson into the picture—a picture Paine was sure had been painted by the KGB—would have taken a long time, planned long ago. And they had no way of knowing that Paine would be assigned to the operation. Or did they?

As if flashing slides in his mind, Paine checked off the major players. Sam Grove? Solid. Charlie Sullivan? A pain in the ass, but solid. Paul Cannon? Ditto. That left someone outside of Europe, someone in Langley.

And who the hell was Al Wilson, anyway?

Suddenly impatient, Paine pulled his car out of the sedate lane and into the no-limit zone, flooring the gas pedal. In a matter of hours he was on the outskirts of Vienna.

Father Robert Bellarmine Beck, SJ, attributed his long life to the three ounces of kirschwasser he drank every morning with his substantial breakfast. While it may have contributed to his longevity, the paralyzing jolt of liquor, along with the bottles of claret at lunch and dinner and the healthy snifters of cognac he drank well into the night, did little for his appearance. His red face was a mass of broken blood vessels; his eyes were cloudy, and until he took his morning refreshment, his hands shook, sending the ash from the first of many Marlboros cascading down the front of his soutane.

Beck may have looked like a mess, but there was nothing slipshod about his mind. At the age of seventy-seven, he remained quick and alert, his brain teeming with knowledge of a thousand arcane subjects and half a dozen languages.

True, toward the end of a boozy evening, he tended to forget what he had been saying, and confused Scottish Gaelic with Erse, but when sober—more or less—there were few men of his age who could boast a mind as sharp.

Born in the United States, he had left it long ago, serving in the Vatican diplomatic corps in a dozen posts, prominent and obscure. At the age of sixty he had retired, but that didn't slow him down. He shuttled around the world doing what he called research for a mammoth tone on the history of his order, staying in Jesuit houses from Fordham to Fiji. Some of his hosts looked forward to his coming, anxious for his good talk, gossip, and bibulous ways; other, more sober priests dreaded his slovenliness, his late nights, and his habit of dipping into the house funds as if they were his personal treasury.

His base, though, was Vienna, in a Jugendstil building on the Kostlergasse, not far from the Viennese flea market. It was there, in a book-, bottle-, and ash-strewn warren, that John Paine found him. The old priest had not seen the young American agent in six years, not since the last class he taught when he had been a guest lecturer at Georgetown. His lectures had been on the history of espionage, a subject dear to his heart—given that the Jesuits had virtually invented the gentle art of spying.

He opened the door, blinked once, and said, as if Paine had just come back from buying a newspaper on the corner: "Just in time; I was thinking about opening a bottle of champagne, and I didn't want to drink it all myself. Good to see you, Johnny."

Paine smiled and shook his hand. "I'm delighted to find you in town, Father."

"Just got back," he said as he ushered Paine into the apartment. "I was with some of the fathers in Crakow. But they threw me out. I'll say one thing for the Polish fathers, though, they certainly know how to live. If their poor parishioners knew, there'd be a revolution. Go into the study." The priest vanished down a dark hallway in search of a bottle.

Paine was puzzled. The entire apartment appeared to be a study. There were books and manuscripts everywhere, worktables awash in weighty tomes and stacks of paper. The study, he decided, was wherever Father Beck was working at any given moment. A cigarette burning in a butt-jammed ashtray suggested that the priest had come to rest in a particular room. Paine excavated an armchair from under a pile of books and two Siamese cats and sat down.

"So that's where the cats got to," said Father Beck, coming into the room. He clutched an icy bottle of Mumm's in one gnarled hand and two glasses in the other.

"Open this for me, will you, John?"

Paine popped the cork and filled the two glasses. Beck drained his with a sigh of pleasure and refilled it.

"Drink champagne every morning, do you, Father?"

"Pooh. Not at all. Today is a special occasion. You've arrived to visit your old professor, and it's a glorious day in the history of Mother Church."

"And what might that be?"

"It's the anniversary of the martyrdom of Saint Eustacius. Hadrian, that old swine, loaded him and his entire family into a metal bull and then built a fire under it. Slow-cooked the saint and all the little saints to be. They did have some elaborate ways of doing away with you back then. Think of all the trouble they went to. Saint Alexandrina was covered with burning pitch. That must have been unpleasant for her, but she was a saint. Just think of the poor bastards who had to apply the stuff!"

"A dirty job," said Paine, "but someone has to—"

"Those poor fellows must have spent all their time trying to think up innovative and entertaining ways to kill Christians. I wonder where the inspiration came from? Was there a whole department in charge of it, or do you suppose that the court torturers took care of the problem? What do you think, Johnny? I must look into that." He made a note on a piece of paper and then lit a cigarette.

"Top up the glasses," he ordered. Paine did as he was told.

"So what brings you to this vile, anti-Semitic

city? The Viennese are so mournful."

"They looked pretty happy to me, Father."

"Nonsense. What in the name of God do you know about it anyway? They're the most mournful, straightlaced people on earth. They haven't gotten over the First World War, never mind the Second. They go back to their *gemütlich* little houses, draw the curtains, and sit there cursing the Jews and the Czar and wish that the Emperor was back. Do you know that at the turn of the century there was a craze—a craze, like Hula Hoops—for suicide. The Viennese tried to outdo each other trying to see who could kill themselves in the most bizarre way. No, hanging or a bullet through the brain wasn't good enough. One of the silly buggers climbed into one of those enormous ornamental pots that stand before the opera house, opened his veins, and waited to fill the damn thing up. That's how they found him, in a bath of his own blood. How they got it out, I'll never know." Father Beck slurped some of his champagne. "I'll tell you something, John Paine. If there had been an Austria during the Roman Empire, instead of a bunch of savages painting themselves blue and wandering around in animal skins, well, the Romans would not have had to look for novel ways of killing the holy martyrs. I'll tell you that." More champagne. "And this longing for the past. It's mad! You know what the most popular boy's name for newborn babies is? Franz-Josef! The name of the old Emperor. They can't get it out of their heads! Stupid bastards." The priest slumped back in his chair. "So. What brings you to my door?"

"Just passing through."

"Do you need a place to stay? I've got plenty of room."

"I wouldn't want to put you out."

"Nonsense. Do you know, I met a lad, a Fulbright scholar, the other day. He's here doing research on something or other. Freud, I think, or maybe it was Engelbert Dollfuss, and he has to leave. And you know why?"

"Why, Father?"

"He's almost got through his entire grant. It was supposed to last him a year, and he's almost spent it all in three months, and you know how?"

"How, Father?"

"Whores!" The priest cackled and slapped his knee. "He told me, this fellow, that there's a house in Vienna where the whores are beautiful and they bring you glasses of champagne in what appear to be salted glasses, like the way those lovely Mexican drinks are served. What are they called, those drinks? Margaritas. Delicious. But it isn't salt. It's cocaine! Can you beat that. Sometimes I think the Viennese aren't so straightlaced, but this lad informs me that the girls are Brazilian."

Paine smiled. "How did this happen to come up in conversation?"

"I was hearing his confession. Poor soul, he

was very guilty-feeling. We fell to talking in the box, you know, and the next thing I knew, my whole hour's duty was up. The most pleasant session I've ever had in the confessional. The old ladies in the church looked at that young man very peculiarly when he came out of the confessional after an hour. You could see them thinking, now, what had that nice, clean-cut boy done that was so awful he had to spend an hour in the confessional? I think it must have been hard on his knees, though."

"If he told you in confession, should you have told me?"

"And why the hell not? It's a good story. The poor lad was very worried about the sex thing and using up all his stipend. I wish I had once had sex in my life, just to see what all the fuss was about."

"There's still time, Father."

"No ... I think that it's better that there's one sin I haven't committed. Seventy-seven years of celibacy is going to have to count for something. Tell me, Johnny, are you still a spy?"

"I never said I was."

"Pooh. Don't be ridiculous. I can remember you at Georgetown, me looking out into the audience and seeing you staring back, and I said to myself, 'Now, there's one of those CIA fellas.' You think I'm joking."

"No," said Paine with a smile. "Just mistaken."

"Then how did you get those little cuts on your

face? Don't tell me you cut yourself shaving, because I won't believe it. You were involved in some kind of rough stuff for that incompetent Agency of yours, weren't you?"

"No. I fell on some gravel."

"Nonsense."

Paine shrugged. "It's the truth."

"No it isn't. But no matter. Now, Father Ricci! There was a spy. He found out more about China than the Chinese." Matteo Ricci was a Jesuit priest who had tried to bring Christianity to China in the sixteenth century. He learned the language—dozens of dialects—became a mandarin and adviser to the Emperor of China and one of the few Westerners until this century to really understand the workings of China and the Chinese mind. "Poor bastard, though. Spent his whole life in China and hardly made a convert. The Society of Jesus in Rome was not happy. Course, they never are."

"How is your work coming?"

Beck waved dismissively. "I'll never be done. I'm up to the suppression of the order, but that has led me into the Bourbon monarchies, and that's a minefield, make no mistake. I want to go to Paris for some research, but those bastards there won't give me a place to stay. You'd think they'd be happy to have a brother of the Society of Jesus under their roof, and a distinguished scholar. The French, they're a miserable people too."

Paine thought of the French soldiers who had

brought him out of Berlin and couldn't bring himself to agree.

"Tell me about your latest adventures, then, Johnny."

"No adventures, Father, not in my field."

"And just what was that again?" Father Beck refilled their glasses. Paine knew well that the old priest had heard his cover story a thousand times, but he took perverse delight in getting him to retell it.

"The international finance business, Father. Aid to developing nations."

"Of course. I forgot. You have philanthropic banker written all over you. And what office politics are you talking about? Someone trying to get rid of you down there at your big bank?"

"You might say that."

"Do you know who? Frederick the Great could teach you something about that, you know. He said that the most important part of warfare was identifying the enemy. That's why the Germans of his era were such good spies—all the soldiering stuff, that came later. Frederick the Great took what the Jesuits had done and built on it. He knew, he knew, the old bastard. Identify the foe first. And it's not always the most obvious target, either. Of course, I don't have to tell you 'bankers' that."

"But what would he have done if the foe was unidentifiable? I mean, in my company we all work together, or at least we're supposed to."

"Afraid of getting stabbed in the back, are you, down there at your company?"

"You might say that."

"But you don't know who by?"

Paine shook his head. "No."

One of the cats jumped onto the desk in front of Father Beck and started lapping at the champagne. "Get away, you miserable animal." The priest slapped at the cat, missed, and knocked over the glass. Wine flooded across the table, soaking a dog-eared manuscript. "Jesus Christ!" He picked up the sodden pages. "Dammit. They're going to be very unhappy with me at the Hertziana Library. This is their damn book, personal recollections of the Prussian ambassador to the court of Clement the Fourteenth— 1773. They've been sending me letters asking for it back for about two years now. Told them I wasn't done with it. Still." He put the manuscript down away from the pool of champagne and poured himself another glass.

"Let me tell you something, Johnny. Nothing's a coincidence. Nothing in espionage, that is. Sorry. Banking. Nothing just happens. Take the Spanish Armada." Father Beck launched into a long and detailed description of the famous naval encounter that destroyed the Spanish fleet in 1588. He spoke as if it happened yesterday. He made references to a dozen names from history, for the most part largely forgotten, but Beck talked as if Alessandro Farnese or the Duke of Medina Sodonia or Charles Howard were about to drop in and join him for a glass of midmorning champagne. The general thrust of the story, though, was that the giant Spanish fleet had been defeated not, as the English liked to think, by superior feats of seamanship, but by espionage and stupidity. "They, the Spanish, I mean, they weren't watching their backs. And who did them in? Not those British. Not at all! But the French. Their allies! If it hadn't been for them, history would be different. England might be a Catholic country today."

"Well, my problems aren't quite so filled with import, Father."

"But they're the only problems you have, Johnny, so you must deal with them. Think logically about who might want to do you in and how, and you'll identify the troublemaker."

Paine nodded. "How can I be sure I have enough information to do that?"

Beck tapped the side of his nose. "You'll know when you know."

"I don't think I know yet."

"Then you will, eventually." He gulped some more champagne. "If you live long enough."

"I told you, Father, it's not a matter of life and death."

"No. Of course not. Drink up. We'll finish this one, have another bottle, and then have some lunch. Some good Austrian pork, some *schweinsbraten* and *knödeln* washed down with some of that disgusting Heurige. A little place in Perchtoldsdorf across the river. Drink up. Drink up."

Father Beck was unimpressed with Paine's small car. "I would have thought that a big banker like you would have had a far more serious car, John. I thought that you financial wizards were supposed to drive big cars so you could impress your clients with how much money you made."

"I'm not that kind of a banker, Father."

Beck's eyes twinkled. "Of course. I was forgetting again. Where did you say your bank was based? It wasn't Langley, Virginia, was it?"

"No, we're right downtown in Washington, D.C."

"But you're still in Rome?"

"That's right."

"I would never have mistaken Italy for an underdeveloped country," said Father Beck. "Third World and all that. But I'm sure it is, if you say so, John. You don't have to explain it to me. I'd never get my old head to understand it."

11

Lunch was long, filling, and alcoholic, and Father Beck talked throughout, never flagging in his consumption of food and drink, and hardly letting up in the conversation. Paine barely spoke, but he didn't mind, quite content to let Beck's talk wander through the ages, vividly re-creating history in a steady stream of gossip, innuendo, and legend. But no matter how far afield he wandered, he always returned to his favorite subject: the secret doings of men and their countries, espionage.

"Things don't change, you know. They don't. Today the human element is gone from the spy game; you bankers know that. Now it's all satellites and what have you, peering down from the heavens watching the whole earth. You think that's new, don't you?"

"It isn't?"

"Pooh. A thousand, two thousand years old, that kind of thing."

Beck shoveled some food into his mouth, and chewed vigorously, speaking between gulps.

"The Romans were so skilled in the art of espionage, the subject peoples, the yahoos in Gaul and Dacia and what have you, could never figure out how the Romans knew when a revolt was coming or when the Huns were going to invade. The Romans always seemed to be there to counter the threat, to fight off the the invader, you know."

Paine smiled. "And they did this with satellites?"

"Pooh. No, of course not. But the people of the empire *thought* they did; that's how effective their intelligence services were. The barbarians said that the Emperor had a magic mirror in his palace and he need only look into it to see the entire Roman Empire. They said that the mirror was mounted on a tall tower that could overlook the whole known world. If that wasn't a satellite, then I don't know what is." He gulped down some Heurige wine.

"The Austrians think this is as good as Beaujolais. Miserable, stupid, anti-Semitic bastards."

Lunch lasted most of the afternoon, and Father Beck was well oiled when Paine managed to get him to leave.

"Maybe we should have one more obstler," said the priest. Obstler was a schnapps made from apples and pears, drunk neat and followed by a glass of cold beer. "Or an Enzian. It's made from flowers, you know. How many times can you claim to have drunk a bouquet of flowers, John Paine?"

"Another time, Father. Why don't you go home and take a little nap, and then we'll have an Enzian later."

"A nap! That's all very well for you spies—sorry, bankers—but there's some of us got to work, you know."

Paine doubted that Father Beck would be doing much work that evening.

"I'll just have a drop of their fine coffee here"—he waved frantically at the waiter—"and then we'll be on our way."

The old priest was glassy-eyed by the time Paine got him to the car. "You know, Johnny, a nap might not be such a bad idea after all."

"You'll feel much better."

"It's my age, you know. I can't do as much as I could when I was younger. I'm slowing down; otherwise I would be bright and ready for work. I'm just too old for a full working day."

Or champagne before lunch, thought Paine. He put the car in gear and pulled out of the parking lot. They hadn't traveled a mile when he realized they were being followed. Four cars back was a Mercedes 190, gray, with Austrian license plates. Two men sat within, and Pain tried, but failed, to make out their features in his rearview mirror. It was an obvious tail, the kind that security forces used to say, "We know you're here and we want you to play by the rules." Paine was disgusted. He hadn't told any-one in Berlin where he was headed, but he gath-ered that the Agency had notified the Austrians and Germans of his general whereabouts. The tail told him a single, chilling fact: the CIA didn't trust him; the long years of confidence in his loyalty and ability had been washed away in the dirty water of a lock on the River Spee.

There was no point in trying to lose them—they probably knew all about him now anyway. He cursed himself for being sloppy, for assum-ing they really were letting him go on vacation.

Natural caution told Paine that he shouldn't drive Father Beck back to his apartment house. Yet the priest, now asleep in the passenger seat, his head lolling back against the headrest, could never make it home on his own. He would have to lead his watchers straight to the old priest's door. Paine made a snap decision: he would leave Vienna immediately, get out of town and cover his tracks—it was the impulse of any trained field agent.

He stopped the car in front of Father Beck's building and gently shook him awake. The priest sat bolt upright and blinked.

"Waiter!" he said.

"Father, you're home."

"So I am. Well, that was a nice snooze, and I don't think I would mind continuing it. Come up, Johnny."

"Not just at the moment, Father. I think I'll

park and take a little walk. Have a look at the beauties of Vienna."

"Miserable city," grumbled Father Beck as he got out of the car. "Populated by miserable people."

In fact, Paine *was* proposing to take a walk. He wanted to lose his followers before returning to his car and making his getaway—it was far easier to lose a tail on foot.

He walked briskly down the Gumpendorfer strasse, making for the Karlsplatz subway station. The gray 190 had vanished, and Paine stopped frequently to survey the sparse crowds on the street, trying to locate his tail. He turned abruptly, doubled back, stopped to admire some shoes in a shop window, and started off again toward the subway. He couldn't be sure, but it seemed that they were leaving him be. They had delivered their message, and that was all that mattered. Still, Paine didn't want to take any chances, so he continued toward the U-bahn station hoping that a couple of quick train changes would put him in the clear. He bought a ticket at a tobacco shop and then plunged into the station, intending to catch the U2 train to Schottenring. Just as he entered the station, he sensed a man at his side. Paine stopped and turned.

He was an overweight, pasty-faced man, his upper lip beaded with sweat, as if he had been running to catch up with him. Paine wondered how he could have missed him.

"Mr. Paine," he said, wheezing slightly as he spoke, "some friends of mine asked me to ask you if you would come and visit them."

"Who are your friends? For that matter, who are you?"

"That is not important."

"To me it is." Paine started to walk away.

The man looked around nervously and whispered: "Mr. Grove said to get in touch with you. He has information for you."

"What information?"

"That I cannot tell you. You must come with me."

The whole thing stunk to high heaven. Paine knew Sam Grove well enough to know that he wouldn't send information through a third party, nothing sensitive at any rate. He also knew that Vienna was lousy with KGB. Much had been made recently about the "new look" in the Soviet secret police; they were supposed to be slicker now, polished and suave. But this specimen appeared to have been cut from the gumshoe cloth of old.

Paine was intrigued. It was one thing to unknowingly walk into a trap, as he had in Berlin. It was another thing altogether to allow yourself to be lured—as long as you went in with your head up and your eyes open.

"Let's go see your friends," he said.

The man seemed relieved. "We'll take the U-bahn. It's only a few stops."

"Fine."

They descended into the complex of tunnels, their footsteps echoing on the tiled walls. Somewhere farther along around a corner, a street musician played a saxophone. The tune sounded like "Stompin' at the Savoy."

Suddenly Paine stopped, turned, and pushed his wrist hard against the messenger's throat, jamming the man back against the grimy wall. He squeaked and gasped, his eyes growing wide with fear.

"Okay. Now tell me what all this is about."

"I don't know anything."

Paine tightened his hold on the man's throat. The man hacked and fought for breath.

"I was told to fetch you."

"Who told you?"

"My superior."

"Who's he?"

The saxophone had stopped playing. Involuntarily the man looked over Paine's shoulder, a tiny gesture that gave Paine enough of a warning to dart away from the knife that was aimed at his back.

The attacker was a young man, a man far younger than Paine. He was dressed in a tattered black T-shirt, dirty jeans, and running shoes. At first Paine thought that the young man was a good samaritan who had come to the aid of a middle-aged man who was being assaulted in the subway. But that kind of thing didn't happen in Vienna. Subway crime was rare—or so the Viennese authorities said—and good samaritans didn't try to kill muggers, just scare them away.

The pasty-faced man fled as Paine turned to confront his attacker. He had tossed away his saxophone, but the bridle that supported it still hung around his neck. Paine wanted to get hold of that, but first he had to get by the knife.

The young man rushed him, waving the knife in short, fast arcs, hoping to catch a piece of Paine and slice. The American forced him back with a sharp kick to the chest and then another to the knife hand. The switchblade flew out of his hand and smacked against the wall. The young man shouted an oath in German and looked worried as Paine moved in for the kill. The knife was too far away for him to reach, but the saxophone was at his feet; he snatched it up. Holding it by the mouthpiece, he waved it menacingly, like a club.

A saxophone? thought Paine. A *saxophone*?

The thug swung, and Paine caught the bell of the instrument and pulled. A sax, he knew, came in three parts, and as the club swung by him, he pulled the lowest part off and threw it back in the man's face. He swung again, smacking Paine in the arm, the valves catching on the sleeve of his shirt. The blow hurt and almost made Paine mad. He snatched the bridle and yanked the man near, bringing his knee up and burying it in his stomach.

The would-be killer collapsed, but Paine hauled him up by the bridle, twisting the cord tight around his neck. The rope bit into the man's greasy skin.

"Who the fuck are you?"

The man shook his head and his eyes bulged. Paine tightened the cord. Blood seeped out from a cut in the man's neck.

"Tell me!"

Again a shake of the head. Paine punched the man hard in the stomach, driving the air up his windpipe, which was all but closed by the noose. The man coughed and gasped and writhed in pain at the same time. "State security," he managed to say, "Austrian."

"And what the hell are you doing?"

"Orders," he said, choking. "Please..."

Paine couldn't kill a member of the Austrian secret service, but on the other hand, it could have been a lie.

"Do you have identification?"

"Please, the rope, loosen it."

Paine tightened it. "Where's your wallet?" He slapped the man's pocket. "Do you have identification?"

The man shook his head. No. Paine relaxed the noose, and the man fell to his knees wretching on the concrete floor, his head bowed, his chest heaving. Foolishly, though, one hand snaked toward the knife. Paine's heel came down hard on the man's wrist and he snapped him back against the wall, slamming his head against the tiles. His attacker went out and crumpled to the floor like a used paper bag.

Quickly Paine went through his pockets and found that the man had been telling the truth: there was nothing more than a few schillings, a pack of cigarettes, and a spare reed for a saxophone. Paine left him where he lay and proceeded to the station platform. He caught a train for Heiligenstadt and varied bus and taxis back to Beck's neighborhood. As he rode along, he kept a sharp lookout for followers but saw none—though they had to be there somewhere. The pasty-faced man was sure to have raised the alarm, and Paine knew that the chances of his getting back into Beck's apartment unseen were slim, and yet he had to go back there. He had to get rid of the car, and to do that, he needed his papers and money, which, foolishly, he had left in his overnight bag in the apartment. He shook his head, saddened by his own sloppy behavior. He was going to have to shape up or pay a very high price for his lack of professionalism. Cunningham would have laughed at him and his dithering ways.

"How far is it to the airport?" he asked his cab driver.

"Not far."

"Is it open late?"

"I don't know."

Paine heard Father Beck's voice: miserable, surly Viennese bastard.

Still, he had done all he had planned. In the event that cab drivers were questioned, then this one would report that the American had expressed interest in the airport, maybe taking a late flight out. It was a story that would slow a good security team down for about fifteen minutes, but it was better than nothing.

"Stop here."

"But you said—"

"Never mind. Stop here."

The driver mumbled a few choice words as he stopped and took Paine's money. He walked the rest of the way, thinking about his encounter in the subway. In the violent life of John Paine, he had been shot at with all manner of firearms, from Saturday night specials to SAMs; he had been on the receiving end of spears, sticks, knives, hatchets, and once—memorably, in Vietnam, in the central highlands—arrows. People had tried to punch him, kick him, claw him, and bite him. But no one, ever, until that day, had tried to kill him with a saxophone.

12

He approached Kostlergasse, the street on which Father Beck lived, cautiously, and again could not identify any surveillance. There were none of those "normal" everyday dead giveaways, like a truck from the electric or telephone company that just happened to be working in the neighborhood. There was no post office van, no innocent-looking street sweeper. There was a police car, but Paine had to assume that was so obvious that it was just a coincidence.

Nothing is ever a coincidence, he heard Father Beck say.

Paine waited for the police car to pass and then walked directly into the building. There was no one in the lobby. Even the gatekeeper's office was empty, the lights out, the door locked.

He avoided the elevator—that was always like walking into a trap—and took the stairs slowly, pausing between landings to listen for footsteps behind him. Silence.

There was no one in the wide, old-fashioned corridor of the building, no sounds, no babies crying, no TV or radio, that suggested that other people lived in the same building.

Paine frowned to himself when he found that the door to Father Beck's apartment was unlocked, slightly ajar. It was always possible that the priest in his befuddlement had forgot to close it behind him, but still Paine didn't like it. As he pushed open the door, one of the cats, leaping at him as if touched with electric current, clawed its way past and out into the hall. Paine had a feeling that the animal was trying to escape from something; he felt himself tense.

Father Beck was in the bedroom, stretched on his bed as if asleep, his glasses, much-repaired with Scotch tape and string, on the night table next to him. The good old man seemed to be wearing a bright red scarf around his neck, a vibrant color contrast to the black of his soutane. Paine saw instantly that he had had his throat cut.

Paine shook his head and walked slowly out of the room, out of the apartment, closing the door firmly behind him. He half hoped, as he headed down the stairs, that he would meet one of them, whoever they were, one of the murderers who had done this to a harmless old man. He wanted to catch one of them and hurt him, make him experience the terror that Beck must have known in his last minutes on earth. Paine wanted to kill.

What the hell were they up to? One thing was plain now, though: whoever was after Paine was playing for keeps. It wasn't just a case of running a loyalty check on an agent they thought to be untrustworthy. Someone wanted Paine out of the way and was prepared to kill the innocent to accomplish that goal. Fine, Paine thought; playing hardball was just fine with him. Now it was personal.

He surveyed the street and saw no one. He walked quickly by his car and hailed a cab on Lehargasse, asking to be taken to the university. There, among a crowd of students, he walked to the Rotenturmstrasse, where he rented a car in a small branch office of Avis under his real name. James Deveraux would vanish that night when Paine had a chance to get rid of his false passport and other documents. Of course, he knew John Paine wasn't going to serve him very well for much longer— he was going to have to assume a new identity, and that would not be easy.

But he couldn't worry about that right now. The important thing was to get out of Vienna, make the trail grow cold, to disappear until he found out just what the hell was going on. He decided to upgrade his transportation a little, choosing a small-model BMW, a common enough car in that part of the world and with a little something extra under the hood in case he needed it. Within twenty minutes he was driving out of Vienna—slowly, though, as rush hour was coming on—headed for safety, wherever that might be.

He stopped for the night in Linz, a city that has the dubious distinction of having been Hitler's hometown, the city he planned to make the art capital of the world—all of the art looted by the Nazis was supposed to have been housed in a single giant museum in the birthplace of the Führer, attesting to Hitler's artistic soul. That, like many other plans of the Reich, never got off the drawing table.

The hotel was, in the Austrian manner, clean, antiseptic, and without soul. The owners were pleasant enough and hardly looked at Paine's passport or face. They provided him with a tasty dinner of schweinbraten, roast pork being the ubiquitous meal in Austria, and a bottle of Heurige and ignored him. He took a double glass of Enzian, Father Beck's beloved schnapps made from alpine flowers, up to his spartan room and went to bed.

He awoke at dawn and discovered he was a wanted man—or rather, James Deveraux was the man whom the Austrian authorities were anxious to question about a murder that had taken place in the capital the day before. Paine sat in the breakfast room of the hotel and tried not to appear too interested in the TV that was on in the corner of the room. A very severe newsreader reported the story without emotion—there's no tradition of news personalities in Europe—telling early risers that a distinguished

American Jesuit scholar had been murdered in his Vienna apartment. A bad picture of Father Beck, obviously taken from a passport, was flashed on the screen, followed by a tape of the exterior of Father Beck's apartment block and the anxious testimony of a neighbor who had seen "a suspicious foreigner" in the area the day before. The newsreader said that James Deveraux was wanted by the police but didn't reveal how the police had come by his name. Paine knew. Someone had told them.

Fifteen minutes later, he was driving out of Linz, headed for Salzburg, the seed of a plan planted in his mind. He had to get out of Austria before the police realized they were looking for John Paine, and he had to get a new set of papers. Heading into Germany was out of the question; that left Italy, just over the border from Austria. Security was lax in Italy, and given that it was just approaching high season, the border crossing points would be thronged with tourists. No doubt the Italians had been asked to look for James Deveraux, but the border guards would be far more interested in processing as many tourists as possible, clearing the backlog to make their own lives a little easier. An American murderer on the run from the Austrian authorities would be the last thing on their minds. He hoped. That still left the problem of the Austrian border patrol. There he would just have to be lucky.

He zoomed past Salzburg and scarcely noticed

the breathtaking beauty of the countryside, pushing on to Innsbruck, where he parked his car and walked away from it, another abandoned vehicle marking his passage through Austria, blazing his trail. It couldn't be helped, though. It was better that they find an abandoned car and know where he had been than to be on the lookout for the car with him in it. He would address the need for transport when he was on the other side of the border.

A poster in the window of a travel agent caught his eye. It advertised a twenty-four-hour tour of northern Italy, including lakes Garda and Iseo. What could be more innocent? It seemed the best way of passing into the country, surrounded by holiday-making tourists, rather than traveling alone on a bus or train.

Paine bought his ticket and was told that a "luxury Pullman-style" bus would be leaving from the office the next morning at six and would return a day later.

"Would I have to come back with the bus or could I stay in Italy?" he asked.

The travel agent looked suspicious. "Are you suggesting that you should receive some kind of reduction?"

"No," said Paine, "I just want to know if I can stay on if I choose to."

"At full fare?"

"Of course."

The travel agent seemed relieved. "You can

do anything you want, sir. It's not the army, you know."

Paine took his ticket, found a hotel, and didn't leave again until it was time to meet the bus the next morning.

There were about fifteen other tourists waiting outside the travel agent when Paine got there just before six, the majority of them Japanese, with a few elderly Americans thrown in. Paine had done his best to dress like a tourist, but he stood out nonetheless, clearly the youngest person in the group.

"You traveling with us, young man?" asked a matronly woman in a white skirt, sneakers, and a cardigan pinned across her chest.

"Yes, ma'am," said Paine.

"You don't mind traveling with us oldsters?" said a man Paine took to be her husband. He was beefy and red-faced and wore a baseball cap. "I'da thought a young guy like you would wanta have a little fun."

"The tour sounds like fun," said Paine lamely.

The man clapped him on the shoulder. "I'm Burt McGee, from Evanston, Illinois. This here's the wife."

Paine shook hands. "John Paine, from New York."

McGee laughed. "Hell, I never could understand how anyone could live in a god-awful town like that. I went there twice for the APGMA convention. That's the American Paper Goods Manufacturing Association—I'm in cardboard—and I couldn't stand it there. Expensive, dirty, all that crime. Hell of a place to raise a family, don't you think?"

"It has its drawbacks."

"What line of work are you in, John? Can I call you John?"

"Sure, Burt."

"What do you do?"

"Banking," said Paine.

"Banks! Banks and lawyers and New York City are just about the three things I hate most. The three things that are the trouble with the country these days. You wouldn't happen to be a lawyer with a bank, would you? If you were a lawyer, then it would be three strikes you're out." McGee guffawed.

"Now, Burt..." cautioned his wife.

McGee slapped Paine on the back. "Now, come on, Maggie, John knows I'm just kidding, don't you, John?"

"Sure do, Burt."

"See, Maggie? But if it'll make you feel any better, John, when we stop for lunch, I'll personally buy you a drink, show you there's no hard feelings. How does that strike you?"

"Good idea, Burt."

"See, Maggie?"

A large bus crept down the narrow road and came to a halt in front of the travel agent. The small group of Japanese who had been watching Burt McGee with much interest turned their gaze from the big American to the big bus.

"Looks like we're gonna get this show on the road," bellowed McGee.

The tour guide was a young, immaculately dressed and coiffed woman who spoke English to the Americans, Japanese to the Japanese, and German to the driver. She looked curiously at Paine. Her name was Miss Muller.

"Taken an eye to you, the little fräulein," said Burt McGee, nudging Paine in the ribs. "Young fella like you shouldn't be alone; maybe something'll develop."

Paine did his best to grin lasciviously. "We'll see, Burt."

Burt McGee and his wife insisted that Paine sit across the aisle from them, and in the two hours it took for the bus to reach the border, Paine learned a great deal about the McGees and their extended family, their past, and their trip to Europe.

"Second honeymoon," said McGee. "First one was in California. Ever been there? Hated Los Angeles and San Francisco. Didn't mind San Diego, though. That was right before I shipped out in forty-four. That was the war, before your time, John."

"Yes, Burt."

"I got three sons, Sammy, Dave, and Burt junior, and two girls, Joanie and Audry."

"Audry's not married," put in Mrs. McGee.

"You married, John? Hell, that's a stupid question, I guess. If you were, then you wouldn't be here all alone."

"Sure wouldn't be, Burt."

"Maybe you and the little fräulein, you know," said Burt with a wink.

Mrs. McGee gave a city-by-city account of their travels—London to Amsterdam to Paris to Munich to Innsbruck, thence to Florence, Rome, and Athens—then switched back to her children. Paine groaned inwardly when she produced a wad of snapshots as thick as the phone book for a good-sized town.

"That's Burt junior," she said, passing a picture across the aisle. "He's in his backyard with his lovely wife, Karen, and their two children, Kara and Jeremy. They're standing next to their pool," she said, as if Paine would have had trouble identifying the clear blue body of water surrounded by lawn.

"Eighty-nine five, they paid for that place. Now it would go for hundred and thirty, hundred and forty. Smart move. You always should buy land. It's the only thing they aren't making any more of. I guess you being a banker, you know about investments and that kind of thing."

"That's what they pay me for, Burt."

"What do you think of three-year money, John?" asked Burt McGee as if he were testing him.

"Depends on your state of liquidity, Burt."

"I figured that."

"And this is Sam with his lovely wife, Janet,

and their two children, Amanda and Abigail. Sam built that deck himself."

"Took him six weeks, working weekends, you know. He's handy that way, like his old man."

"He's in insurance and doing awfully well."

"It's a good field to be in," said Paine, wishing they were at the border. Facing the Austrian police would probably be preferable to the McGees and their sons and their lovely wives. He was relieved when Miss Muller announced that she would be collecting the passports for the border control. She smiled when she took Paine's, setting off another bout of leering and winking from Burt McGee.

There was a mile-long line of cars, trucks, and buses waiting to cross from Austria into Italy. Paine didn't know, and had no way of finding out, if this meant that the guards were being extra careful, looking for him, or if this was business as usual. Suddenly he regretted his decision to take the tour bus: he couldn't look more obvious—or so it seemed to him—sitting there surrounded by quiet, elderly Japanese and the crew-cut McGee. For a moment he thought of getting off the bus, but that would have been foolish. All he could do was sit and wait and hope that the Austrians were still looking for James Deveraux.

Miss Muller got back on the bus and unclipped the microphone and spoke first in rapid Japanese and then in English.

"We will be passing into Italy shortly. Our

first stop will be the city of Bolzano, where we will have lunch and you will have two hours for sight-seeing. From there we will head south to the town of Trento, where we will spend the night."

Burt McGee clapped his hands. "Lunch! Good. Then I can buy you that drink I promised you, John."

"I'm counting on it, Burt," said Paine as the bus rolled into Italy.

Bolzano had a more German flavor to it than Italian, a fact that didn't escape Burt McGee.

"Hell, feels like we never left Austria."

"It only became part of Italy after the First World War," explained Miss Muller. She was sitting at the head of the American table in the tourist trap restaurant they had been booked into by the tour company. The decor and the food were Tyrolean, stuffed boars' heads and *gemütlich* carved wood all over the place, and the waiters wore leather lederhosen but spoke to one another in voluble Neapolitan-accented Italian. They were obviously impoverished exiles from the South who had come to the prosperous North to find work.

Burt McGee, overjoyed at finding "real Eyetalians" in the restaurant, asked one of them if he had ever heard of Joe DiMaggio. The waiter smiled, said something obscene in the Neapolitan dialect, and fled.

After lunch, Paine approached Miss Muller while McGee hovered in the background resisting his wife's efforts to pull him away for their allotted two hours sight-seeing.

"Miss Muller . . ."

"Yes, Mr. Paine?"

"I don't want to offend anybody, but if it's okay with you, I think I'll be leaving the tour here."

Miss Muller looked slightly annoyed. "Is something not to your satisfaction? Have I done something wrong?"

"No, no, it's not that. It's just that, well, I think you can see that I'm a little out of place in this group. I think I'm making people uncomfortable."

"Nonsense, Mr. Paine."

Paine smiled. "Well, then, it's I who feel uncomfortable, taking a senior citizens' tour like this."

"*I'm* not old, Mr. Paine."

"Yes, but it's your job. I really think it would be better if I just took off here."

Miss Muller looked disappointed and she shrugged. "As you wish, Mr. Paine. I'll have Heinrich take your bag off the bus."

Paine was relieved. The McGees had gone off to look at old Bolzano, leaving him the opportunity to make a clean, quick getaway. By the time the sightseers returned to the bus, Paine was on a train to Venice.

"Musta struck out with the fräulein," said Burt McGee.

13

"Merv," said the man at the bar, "Merv Holst."
He put his hand out, and he and Paine shook.

"Burt," said Paine, "Burt McGee."

"Good to meet you, Burt."

"Likewise, Merv."

"So what brings you to Venice, Burt?"

"Just traveling around. Always wanted to see
Venice. Hell of a place, isn't it?"

"I never seen anything like it," said Merv
Holst. "I didn't want to come, you know. I said,
'Europe? In July?' It'll be hot, crowded, expensive. I told my daughter—I'm traveling with my
little girl and a friend of hers—let's go someplace summery, you know, like Hawaii. But
Courtney insisted, and here we are. And it's just
like I said it would be, hot, crowded, and expensive, but it's been a hell of a trip so far, and
it's gonna be hard for Courtney's mother to top
this. Let me tell you." He sipped his drink.
"We're divorced."

John Paine had chosen Merv Holst carefully. He had been to a dozen hotel bars in Venice looking for the right person: a white American male about his age, preferably alone, and who liked to take a drink. Holst was a little older than Paine, at least Paine guessed he was, but other than that, he was perfect. John Paine was going to steal his identity. In his wallet he already had four photographs of himself, taken in one of those automatic booths, and if all went well, by the next morning at ten he would have ceased to be John Paine or James Deveraux and become Mervyn Holst. The best thing about it was that no one—not Holst, not the U.S. passport office, not the CIA—would know about it except John Paine.

They were sitting in the cool, dim, tasteful bar at the Hotel Danieli, one of the great hotels of Venice, sipping their expensive drinks, and in the manner of American travelers the world over, had gotten talking. Paine probed gently and did his best to remember everything Holst told him.

He was an engineer from San Rafael, California, divorced, one kid, a mortgage, a dog, a cat, and a Toyota that needed some work done on its brakes. A graduate of Golden Gate University, a tennis player, a Giants fan; in short, Mr. Average.

Perfect, thought Paine.

"How 'bout another, Merv?"

"Don't mind if I do. The kids are in bed, thank

God. Tomorrow I'm taking them to the beach. I think they had enough of old churches and art and stuff today. Courtney is real artistic, but she's thirteen, you know. She likes to run around and have fun. So tomorrow's an easy day for me. Sit on the beach and drink some lousy Italian *cerveza*. Is that what they call beer, like in Spanish?"

"They call it *birra*."

"*Birra*," said Holst. "Hell, that's easy to remember. What are you drinking, Burt?"

"Scotch."

"Me too. Hey, two more please."

"You staying here, Merv?"

Holst looked around the elegant bar and the opulent lobby. "I wish. This place costs about four hundred bucks a night. No, I don't have that kind of dough. You?"

"Me neither," said Paine. "I'm at a place called the Fontana. Nice enough. Eighty-five or so a night. Not bad. Clean."

"We got rooms at the Albergo Grand. Right around the corner. I just came in here to get cool. This place has air-conditioning, but I don't think the rest of Italy has discovered it yet."

Holst had a point. It was mid-July in Venice, and the city was baking under an unrelenting Adriatic sun. The nights weren't much cooler either, even with the breeze off the lagoon. The crowds that thronged Venice's narrow streets didn't help the general level of comfort much either.

"Hell of a thing, them building a city out here in the middle of the bay. We had a tour guide today who said that the whole city is built on wooden piles. Now, I'm an engineer, and I know that something like that isn't easy to pull off. This whole damn city is going to sink someday, or that's what they tell me. Makes sense from an engineering point of view. Sure will be a shame when it goes. I'm glad Courtney and Kimberly—that's her friend—could see it. Hell, I'm glad *I* could see it."

"Me too. Let me get the next round."

Holst hesitated a moment, then gave in. "Hell, it's an easy day tomorrow."

"You a superstitious man, Merv?"

"Naww, not really. I mean, I don't walk under a ladder unless I can help it. You?"

Paine did his best to look sheepish. "No. I mean, at least I didn't think I was, but today when I was checking in to my hotel, they told me my room number was 1313, and I felt a little funny about that."

Holst laughed. "Well, it does bother some people. You know, when they put up a building, they don't have a thirteenth floor. Goes straight from twelve to fourteen; trouble is that there's *still* a thirteenth floor, no matter what they call it. But you're right, you notice it when it happens to you, like with your room number and all. I'm in 209, and that seems nice and safe to me."

"Lucky you."

Holst slipped two drinks ahead of Paine—just as he planned—and the scotch loosened his tongue. In the next hour Paine learned that Holst still loved his wife—although she was a "class-A bitch on wheels"—and that Courtney needed to have a stable home life. Paine further learned that building and drainage ordinances in Marin County were "for shit," that Merv had lost a bundle in the stock market dive a couple years back, and that he couldn't get laid in San Francisco. "The AIDS thing, you know, it's made all the bitches paranoid."

At one o'clock, when the Danieli bar closed, Holst and his newfound friend Burt McGee staggered out into the quiet streets of Venice, almost deserted at that late hour—Venice traditionally is an early-to-bed town.

"Christ," said Holst, "am I shitfaced."

John Paine didn't think he was drunk enough, not yet. "Tell me, Merv, have you ever had an Italian drink called grappa?"

Holst stared glassily at his companion. "I dunno; what is it?"

"It's hard to explain; maybe you should try some."

Holst shrugged. "What the hell, it's an easy day tomorrow," he said for the fourteenth time that night.

Finding a late night bar in Venice is no easy task, and Paine was afraid that Holst would sober up as they trailed along narrow streets and over the steep bridges that span the canals.

At a quarter to two in a side street in the Dorsoduro section of the city, they found a bardance club, which catered to the few late night reveling tourists not exhausted by a full day of sight-seeing.

Paine ordered grappa, a ferociously strong drink which the Italians like to compare to cognac—a kind comparison to grappa, which, though distilled from grapes, could never be mistaken for a fine French brandy. Luckily Holst liked it.

He shivered as the first belt went down. "Christ," he said hoarsely. "That is some helluva drink."

"Another?" suggested Paine.

Holst had another.

"I can't tell you how glad I am that I bumped into you, Burt. I get tired of being alone or with the kids. You know how it is; occasionally you have to be with someone your own age. It seems everybody I met on this trip has been a senior citizen, a college kid, or just a, you know, a kid. Like Courtney."

Paine topped up his drink.

"You oughta come to the beach with us tomorrow," Holst managed to say. "Take a day off from the churches and museums and shit like that."

"Sounds like fun. What time you heading out?"

"Probably round eleven, something like that."

"I'll come by your hotel."

"Great," said Holst, slurping down the last of his grappa.

At four-fifteen, Paine loaded Merv Holst into a water taxi and they motored through the canals to the Grand Hotel. There Paine consigned his very drunk friend into the arms of the hotel concierge, mission partially accomplished.

At eight-thirty the next morning, Paine breezed through the busy lobby of the hotel, found room 209, and neatly picked the lock of the door using the tweezers of his Swiss Army knife.

Within the darkened room he found exactly what he expected. Merv was stretched on the bed heavily asleep, his mouth open, snoring slightly—Paine knew from experience that there was no sleep more profound than one induced by half a bottle of poisonous grappa. Working swiftly, he found Holst's wallet; containing his passport, driver's license, and credit cards, pocketed them, and let himself out of the room, Holst sleeping blissfully unaware through the operation that had taken less than a minute.

The thieves hadn't started their busy day's work of fleecing the natives, so the police station on the Calle Pestrin was quiet. The carabinieri were polite and understanding yet maddeningly slow.

"I had my wallet stolen," Paine told the man at the desk.

The cop on the desk didn't speak English, but

he knew why American tourists visited Italian police stations on beautiful summer mornings.

"Ah," he said, and disappeared for five minutes, returning with a police lieutenant who spoke English.

"I had my wallet stolen," Paine repeated.

"Unfortunate," said the police lieutenant. "Please tell what happened. Please." He showed Paine to a seat in front of a metal desk on which stood a manual typewriter. The cop typed as Paine slowly told his story, pausing every so often to allow the policeman to catch up or to unjam the keys of the old manual. When Paine was done, the cop typed steadily for ten minutes, then whipped the document out of the machine.

"You were walking in the Piazza San Marco when you were approached by two young children carrying sheets of newspaper. They pressed the newspaper against you and begged for money. Correct?"

"That's correct."

"They were Gypsies, you know. We're not allowed to say they were Gypsies—that would be considered racist—but they come over from Yugoslavia and prey on the tourists." The lieutenant paused to light a cigarette. Paine shifted uneasily, aware of the passage of time and the sleeping Merv Holst.

"So," the cop continued, "Mr. Holst, you went to a *caffè* to have a coffee when you realized that your wallet was missing, containing a U.S. passport number 1267890Z, two hundred thousand lire, three hundred dollars, a Visa card from the Bank of America, and a driver's license. Is so?"

"Yeah, goddammit."

"Sign please."

Paine signed the document, and the cop stamped it vigorously. "One copy for you. One copy for our files."

"Now what the hell do I do?"

The man shrugged. "The money is gone, of course. Sometimes the documents are found by the police in garbage cans. We will return to you them, but it is not wise to wait. Now you must go to the American consul and get an emergency replacement passport. You show them this form. It is very simple."

Paine stood. "Hell of a way to spend your vacation. I was supposed to take my little girl to the beach today."

"On behalf of the city of Venice, sir, I apologize and hope you will not judge us by this unfortunate incident."

"Forget it," said Paine.

The bureaucrats at the American consulate on the Riva degli Schiavoni were as slow as the Italian cop but far less pleasant. An assistant consul examined the typed police statement closely, as if it might have been a forgery, asked Paine a couple of intrusive questions, and then disappeared into a back room for what seemed like an hour but was, in fact, only fifteen minutes. It was long enough for Paine to crank up his irate tourist act and point out to a secretary that he, an American taxpayer, paid her salary and the salary of everyone else in the plush suite of offices. The secretary flashed him a look that read "I could give a shit" in every known language.

Finally the consul returned with the emergency passport with one of the passport pictures clipped to it. The face was crumpled with the press of the official seal of the State Department.

"Forty dollars," said the consul.

"I don't have forty dollars. I was robbed, remember."

"Oh." The consul returned to the inner office for another ten minutes, then reappeared. "We can't issue a replacement passport here, only this temporary one. You'll have to pick up the real thing in Milan. But you'll have to pay the forty bucks there before they give it to you."

"Fine."

"Have a nice day," said the consul.

Holst was still asleep when Paine broke into his hotel room again. He replaced the documents and the wallet and let himself out.

Courtney Holst woke her father at twelve, thoroughly miffed that her father had overslept.

"Daddy," she said irately, "you *promised*."

Holst felt terrible. His head pounded, his stomach heaved, his hands trembled, and he could barely recall his drinking companion of the night before.

"Daddy?"

"Courtney, why don't you go and play in a canal, honey."

"Very funny," said Courtney.

"Look, go away for a few minutes while I take a shower so we can head out to the beach." All Merv Holst wanted to do was go back to bed and die, but he was aware of his duties as a rival parent. He swung himself out of bed, lurched into the bathroom, and showered. Twenty-five minutes later, he was crossing the lagoon with his little girl and her friend, having forgotten Burt McGee and his invitation to the beach. Holst would never again, in his entire life, drink grappa.

Before Holst got to the beach, John Paine, now in possession of papers attesting to his identity as an engineer from California named Mervyn Holst, boarded the first-class *ràpido* train for Milan. At four that afternoon he was issued with a spanking new American passport and he officially became one of two Mervyn Holsts on the continent of Europe.

14

Internal security at the CIA was no one's idea of a dream assignment, despite the power and authority the head of the department wielded. Mark Berghold did not ask for the appointment, and neither did he relish the task of policing the twenty thousand employees of the Central Intelligence Agency, constantly suspicious of their loyalty, constantly on the alert for the slightest sign that one of the vetted agents was, in fact, working for the other side. No one liked the agents of the Internal Security Division, but that didn't bother Berghold, not at all; what preyed on his mind was the possibility that he might make a mistake, suspect and destroy a solid agent or, worse, allow a tainted agent to slip through the security unit he commanded. He didn't like the look of the Paine case at all.

He had reviewed the files on Paine carefully and thoroughly, learning all there was to know about the man, or rather, all that the CIA knew about one of their star agents, and that was a considerable amount of information.

"There's nothing in Paine's profile that says he's been turned," he concluded.

Cunningham nodded. "He hasn't been."

"We don't know that for sure," said Tom Weinberg.

"He's solid," insisted Cunningham.

"How can you be so sure?" Bill Mitchell was Berghold's executive officer, a giant, beer-swollen man who had come over to the CIA from the FBI and had never lost the look of a fed gumshoe. He was the first to admit that he was no genius, but he had an enviable knack for taking Berghold's cerebral ideas and orders and translating them into rough action. If an agent's loyalty was in question, then Mitchell would ride herd on him until he cracked and confessed or was given a clean bill of health. Mitchell's bulk and strong-arm tactics had earned him the unlovely nickname "Bluto."

"I'm sure," said Cunningham.

"That's a lot of bullshit. Sorry, Mark."

Berghold didn't like obscenity.

"Think what you want, Bill, but I'm telling you the man is solid."

"If he's solid, how do you explain Wilson? And the priest in Vienna?"

"John wasn't involved in the priest's murder. It's pretty obvious to me that he's been set up."

"By who? Us? Them? What kind of bullshit is that? Sorry, Mark. It's not us. And why would they? No, what's fuckin' obvious to me—sorry—is that Wilson found out about him, and the priest found out about him, and they had to go."

"That's not the way Paine would handle things," said Cunningham.

"The fuck he wouldn't. The guy's a killer. He'd kill at the drop of a hat if he had to. He cut Wilson's fuckin' thumb off. Sorry, Mark."

"Kevin, is he still in Austria?" Berghold lit a cigarette and sat back in his tall-backed chair.

Cunningham laughed. "How the hell should I know?"

"What's your gut feeling?"

"No."

"I didn't think so."

"Pull him in," said Bluto, "then we'll find out what the hell is going on."

This time Berghold laughed. "It's not quite that easy, Bill. Paine's pretty clever."

"He can be got." Bluto's voice rang with assurance.

"Who's going to get him," asked Cunningham derisively, "you?"

"Fuck yes." Bluto winced and looked at his boss, who waved away the obscenity as if fanning away a bad smell.

"I think Bill has the right idea. I think it's time we had a talk with John Paine. Mr. Endicott would like this whole thing cleared up. And the Austrians are upset about the priest."

Cunningham was about to say, "Fuck the Austrians," but stopped himself.

"Paine won't be caught until he wants to be caught," he said instead. "I've seen the man work. He could hide in this room and you wouldn't find him."

"Bullshit! Sorry. He's in nice civilized Europe, Cunningham. It's not the Central fucking Highlands—sorry, Mark—and this is the Central Intelligence Agency, not the Keystone Kops. If we can't find him, then no one can."

"Okay, Bill," said Berghold, "you want to give it a shot?"

"Fuckin' A."

"Kevin, I'd like you to liaise with Bill. You analyze any information Bill reels in."

Before Cunningham could object, Bluto shook his head. "No way, Mark, no way. I don't want Cunningham on the operation; he's a better friend to Paine than he is to . . ." Mitchell shook his head again. "Forget it."

Kevin Cunningham had gone white with rage and he twisted in his wheelchair. "My loyalty is in doubt now, is that right, Bluto?"

Mitchell colored, a deep, angry scarlet. "Don't call me that."

"I think Bill might have a point," said Weinberg soothingly. "It would be a terrible conflict for Kev. We should never ask someone to betray a friend."

Graham Greene's famous line flashed through Cunningham's mind: "If I had to choose between betraying a friend or betraying my country, I hope to God I would have the courage to choose my country."

Cunningham looked at the men in the room and realized, sadly, that his friend, John Paine, had already been betrayed by his country.

"Bill," ordered Berghold, "go. Go to Europe and find him."

"Yes, Chief."

"We've asked the Germans, the Austrians, the Italians, and the Swiss to see if they can find the last known whereabouts of John Paine or his alias James Deveraux. We should have that information by this afternoon," said Weinberg. "That'll be your starting point, Bill."

Bluto assumed the confident look he took on when he was about to utter what he thought was a bon mot. "Austria, Italy, Switzerland, Germany, eh? What happens if he went East? What if he's sitting in Moscow right now having a little snort of vodka and picking out his place in the Kremlin Wall?"

"Well, fuck you, asshole," exploded Cunningham.

"Sorry, Mark," said Bluto.

"Coyote is off-line, and so is Sentry," said Endicott.

The Director of Central Intelligence rubbed his eyes. "Gone? Are you sure?"

"As sure as we can be. Sam Grove thinks that he's confirmed Sentry."

"So we've lost our switchboard in East Germany."

"I'm sorry, Lucian, but it seems that's the case."

"That is going to make our job just a touch more difficult," said George Rafferty.

"Paine?" said the Director.

"Who the hell else?" Rafferty had the innocuous title of CIA Head of Research, but next to the DCI, he was probably the most important man in the Langley headquarters. Far from being at the command of dozens of burrowing bookworms, Rafferty collated and analyzed all intelligence—human and satellite—that flooded into the Langley headquarters of the Central Intelligence Agency. It came from many sources, from billion-dollar satellites silently orbiting above the earth to the sharp eyes of a bedouin leading his pack animals past an Iraqi missile installation; Rafferty commanded the knowledge of bar girls in Tokyo, butlers in Istanbul, black marketeers in Mozambique, university lecturers in Crakow, a myriad of spies and informers, some working for money; others for ideology, some for the fun and danger of it. Rafferty answered questions, an invaluable tool in intelligence—if you held the answers in your hand, then you held power.

The DCI didn't look happy. "Let's recap. Paine is out there, out of control, working against us."

"We don't know that," said Endicott.

"He's certainly a loose cannon," put in Rafferty.

"And Internal Security is looking for him?"

"As of today, Lucian. Mark has a team headed for Europe. We have guaranteed cooperation from all the allies involved."

"So we won't know anything till we find him," said the DCI with an air of finality.

"He'll be able to answer a lot of questions." Answers were Rafferty's obsession.

"Find him," said the Director of Central Intelligence. "Thank you, gentlemen."

The head of research and the head of the European desk rose. "Just one more thing," the Director asked.

Both men stopped.

"Is it true that Paine cut the thumb off of this, this Wilson?"

Both men nodded.

"And what do you make of that?"

"Barbarism," said Endicott.

George Rafferty smiled. "On the contrary, Arthur, I would have said that it was an inspired bit of improvisational fieldcraft."

Endicott frowned. "It's not the way we did things in the old days."

"In the old days," repeated Rafferty, giving the distinct impression that the old days were dead and gone.

15

In the nineteen years since that hot summer day when a "friendly" mine exploded under him in Kontum, Kevin Cunningham had learned how to live with his disability. It had not been easy, going from a powerfully built, athletic young man, a tough, almost obsessively self-reliant kid, to a twisted, disabled adult dependent on friends and family for the simplest function. At first he had gone through the classic phases of rage and despondency, hating the people around him who were whole and healthy, rejecting his loved ones—an extended Irish-American family, his fiancée, his friends, even, for a while, John Paine. Somehow, though, he came to realize that this was the hand life had dealt him and that there was nothing else to do but to make the best of it. First he worked on what was left of his body, developing his good arm until it could do the work of two. Before the accident, he had been right-handed; now he wrote, threw, and fired a gun left-handed. In the old days he had been a jock, far more at home on the playing field than in a library, but the mine had spared his mind, and he realized that his brain was virtually the only part of him in perfect working order. He set out to make it even better.

He had gone straight from high school into the service, so he started his education anew, feeling foolish and self-conscious in his wheelchair when he started as a freshman at Northern Virginia Community College. He was older than the other students in the class, he was the only disabled—he was pretty sure he was the only person in the class who had ever killed a man, but that didn't enter into it—but, he realized, he was also smarter; smarter and more driven. The teenagers who attended school with him were bored, going through the education motions because it was expected of them, biding their time 'till something better came along. Cunningham's age and circumstances told him that there wasn't a moment to lose, that Northern Virginia Community College was it, it was life, it was his last best chance. It wasn't Harvard or Yale, but it was all he had, and he determined to make the best of it.

Cunningham, to his surprise, came to love school, knowledge, reading, books. When one of the teachers handed out an assignment on a Friday and the other students rolled their eyes and cursed, Cunningham was delighted at the idea of spending hours in the library, prospecting like a gold bug for a single nugget of information, assembling his facts, presenting his point of view, defending his position. It was almost a military exercise, and to Cunningham, almost as invigorating.

When other students got their papers back covered in red ink, they rolled their eyes again, thought uncharitable thoughts about their professor, glanced at the grade, and tossed the paper in a drawer, never to be looked at again. Cunningham read and reread the criticisms and took them to heart.

Some people are lucky enough to meet a great teacher, a guide into the world of learning, a Rosetta stone to translate the dense texts of academics, and Professor Ostrowsky was his. She was a sad-looking woman, a refugee from Poland, holder of a raft of degrees from European universities now far behind the Iron Curtain. She had fled her country in 1939 and had never returned, marrying an American and raising a bunch of towheaded American kids. But there was still a strong air of *mittel* European learning and culture about her, a heavy Polish accent and a hint that she was still more at home discussing the world of ideas in French or German than English. She, like Cunningham, had returned to academia late in life. Had she put her mind to it earlier on, instead of being a good American housewife, he was sure that she would have been a full professor at a prestigious American seat of learning. But Northern Virginia Community College was her lot in life and she was content with that—but she was determined that it would not be the end of the line for Kevin Cunningham.

At the end of one of her classes in international relations, she had asked him to stay behind.

"Mr Cunningham," she said, looking over the top of her half-frame glasses, "perhaps you can tell me what you are doing here?"

Cunningham felt his blood chill. He knew there was nothing wrong with his work—Professor Ostrowsky handed out A's with monotonous regularity—so he could only assume that she was going to give him some trouble about the role he had played in the Vietnam War— the year was 1974, and there was still an undercurrent of resentment against vets. Once, he had been asked how many babies he had slaughtered.

"I'm not sure what you mean, Professor Ostrowsky."

"The assignment for this week . . ."

" 'Trace the origins of the rise of the Third Reich from the Treaty of Versailles to the elections of 1932.' "

"Correct. I have a paper here by one of your classmates, Henry—though he prefers to be known as Hank—Simmons. The first line reads: 'The Germans were beat really bad in the First World War and wanted to get even . . .' "

Cunningham smiled. Hank Simmons was a nice kid but clearly no genius, more interested in his girlfriend than in his studies.

"It seems a pretty straightforward way of putting it, Professor."

"'The diktat of 1919 sowed the seeds of the German discontent, which would bear the bitter fruit of the Second World War twenty years later...'" Ostrowsky glared at him. Cunningham blushed—he hated to have his own words quoted to him.

"Do you see the difference, Mr. Cunningham?"

"Different language for the same sentiments, Professor."

Now Ostrowsky smiled. "That's not the point. Mr. Simmons's conception of history is based on the football field or the *Boy's Book of Battles*. You understand the complex issues involved here. I think you should consider a better place of education. There's nothing here for you, not at 'good old NVCC.'" Cunningham could hear her words bristling with quotation marks. "I have arranged for you to meet a friend of mine, Sylvester Wolman... You recognize the name?"

"Of course." Wolman was the author of a dozen texts on European diplomatic history, with an accent on the Soviet Union since the Second World War.

"He is chairman of the history department at Johns Hopkins, and I have convinced him that you might be a worthy student there."

"There's nothing in my background that says Johns Hopkins, Professor." Or my bank account, he thought.

"You have a good mind and you need training. Training you can't get here. Sylvester says that—if he approves of you, and you are prepared to do some hard reading this summer—you could join the freshman class at Hopkins in the fall. On a scholarship. A full scholarship, Mr. Cunningham. It's quite a challenge; do you accept?"

In 1974 Cunningham was almost twenty-six years old. The idea of entering a prestigious college four years after most people his age had graduated was a daunting one. He would have to undergo the giggles and the stares again, the sense of being a freak, of not belonging. Still, the chance was too good to pass up . . .

"Yes, Professor, I think I do."

"Good."

Cunningham did four years of college in three, and a Ph.D. in two, graduating covered with academic honors in 1979. It was a remarkable year: his degree, his employment by the CIA, and his marriage to a fellow graduate student; John Paine, home from the intelligence wars, had been his best man. Paine had been pleased by his friend's good fortune, his young bride, Jenny, but most of all, by Kevin Cunningham's employment.

"It'll be nice to know that someone back at Langley is on my side."

"John, I'm an analyst on the Russian desk. How can I watch your back?"

"It's just nice to know you're there, Kev. Besides, I have a feeling the Russian desk is going to be busy. And so will I."

Cunningham nodded. Paine didn't know, and Kevin couldn't tell him, but there was something in the air. The day after Christmas, the Russians invaded Afghanistan. Paine infiltrated the country in January 1980.

But that had been nine years before. Cunningham had reclaimed his life, built something out of his tortured body and tragic past. Now, though, he saw the Agency he worked for, defended, and admired trying to destroy his best friend, the man who had saved his life. Cunningham was at home, in his study, dozing over a book and a glass of scotch on the rocks, the air conditioner humming, when the phone rang. It was late. Jenny, an associate professor of history at George Washington University, had gone to bed, so Cunningham grabbed the phone on the second ring lest it wake his wife. He heard the airy sound of a long-distance call.

A voice: "Do you know who this is?"

Cunningham felt his heart pound in his chest. "Yes."

"Good." The line went dead.

Cunningham unlocked a desk drawer and slipped a short-barreled Smith & Wesson .38 Military Airweight revolver into the saddlebag of his wheelchair. He glanced at his watch as he wheeled himself out of the study, rolling silently over the terra-cotta floor of the apartment through the wide door of his bedroom. His wife slept still and calm under the sheet. He touched her cheek and she awoke, groggy and slightly disoriented; he could see her face clearly in the light thrown by the street beyond their bedroom window.

"What is it?"

"Something's come up," he said, hoping his voice sounded soothing. "It's probably nothing, but I have to go into the office."

"What time is it?"

"'Bout one o'clock. Just go back to sleep. I'm sorry I woke you, but I didn't want you to wake up and find me not here."

"Do you want me to drive you?" Jenny half rose from the bed.

"No. Just go back to sleep." Cunningham rolled down the corridor of the apartment building and took the elevator to the basement parking lot. He had a new Ford converted for his use. There was no front seat where the driver sat, and a lift hooked on the outside of the car, hoisting his chair up and into the car, locking behind the wheel. Like every red-blooded American teenager, Kevin Cunningham had loved cars and had spent long hours in high school debating the merits of every exotic machine on the road. Back then, when he had driven a beat-up Ford, he had sworn that by the time he was thirty, he would have a Ferrari—here he was well past thirty and he still had a Ford. Ferrari didn't adapt cars for disabled use.

He drove through the quiet Washington streets, his eyes flicking up to the mirror every few seconds trying to make a tail. No cars followed; behind him was nothing but black highway. He crossed the river into Virginia and threaded his way along the freeway toward Arlington, keeping things slow and steady, letting the late night shift workers pass him as they zoomed home on the open road. He had more than an hour to make his rendezvous.

He cruised the streets in Arlington, passing a couple of bored cops who didn't give him a second glance, wandering the streets, the numbered ones South Twenty-third, South Twenty-fourth, and the named, Glebe, Norwich, Hudson, wending his way through residential neighborhoods and commercial, curving through the thicket of ugly hotels and high rises in Crystal City, wasting time and watching his ass. He wasn't being followed—he was sure of that—and the chances were good that not even Bluto had tapped his phone yet, but it was wise to take precautions. No one knew that better than Kevin Cunningham, expect perhaps for John Paine.

Years before, they had set up this communications system, a dead phone at a shopping center in Arlington where Paine could call if there was ever need to talk to his friend unobserved. When Paine had first mentioned it to him, Cunningham had thought that he was being overdramatic, overcautious, or perhaps even paranoid, his nerves stretched too tight by years in the field. Paine knew that to set up a situation like this was in direct contravention of Agency orders, and Cunningham further knew that if he or Paine was caught, then the evidence would look bad—for both of them.

He could imagine Bluto's direct, blunt line of questioning.

"So you got back-channel communications with Paine. How come?"

"In case he ever wanted to get in touch with me..."

"What's he got to hide, Cunningham?" Or, for that matter, the unspoken question: what did Cunningham have to hide? If he was caught communicating with his friend in this way, then they could only make the assumption that he and Paine were in this together, whatever "this" was.

The plan was simple enough. The number—unless it had been changed—would ring one hour and thirty minutes after the initial call. The phone booth was in the parking lot of a Giant Supermarket, and the lot was the size of a football field—plenty of room to allow Cunningham a clear view of anyone headed in his direction. Of course, the act of receiving a phone call in the middle of the night in a deserted parking lot would be a tough one to explain.

"You see, Bluto, it's like this. I had to pick up

a few things at the Giant and decided I would make a few calls..." There was no way to explain it. Cunningham, Paine, and Bluto knew that. So the important thing was not to get caught doing it.

The phone booth looked like a lighted beacon in the middle of the field of black asphalt. Some cars were parked near the doors of the supermarket, but the nearest bit of cover to the booth itself was a tangle of shopping carts. Cunningham maintained something of a proprietary interest in the upkeep of this particular phone booth. Twice he had called the phone company to report that it had been vandalized, demanding that something be done about fixing it. The booth had been chosen with care—it was wide enough to admit his chair.

The phone rang more or less to the second. He let it ring three times, then picked it up.

"Good to hear your voice, buddy," said Paine.

"Likewise."

"Kevin, what the hell is going on?"

Cunningham sighed. "John, you tell me."

"Someone is setting me up."

"I figured. Why?"

"That's what I'd like to know."

"John, that's what *everybody* would like to know."

"What's the mood there? What are people saying?"

"The mood is ugly. Some—the majority—are saying you've gone over. They say that guy, what's his name, Wilson, figured out you were a double and you killed him. They didn't like that stuff with the thumb..."

Paine sighed. "I didn't like it much myself, but I figured they would need it to ID him. I would say that it shows that I was solid and that Wilson was the double, not me."

"And the priest in Vienna."

"Kevin, you know I had nothing to do with that."

"Sure, *I* know. But they're saying that he, too, figured out your position."

"Who? Who's they?"

"Bluto, for one..."

"That jerk."

"Endicott can't make up his mind. Weinberg won't say—"

"Typical."

"—but I think he's leaning towards the Paine-is-a-traitor theory."

"If Bluto has been called in, then that means that Internal Security is up in arms. What does Berghold say?"

"You know him. On one hand this, on the other hand that. He'll play it straight down the middle until there's evidence. He's got a mind like a lawyer, or a judge. Innocent till proven guilty, you know."

"The DCI?"

Cunningham laughed. "John, things haven't changed here that much. The DCI doesn't drop by my cubicle to tell me what his thinking is on the Paine case."

"You aren't picking up any scuttlebut around the water cooler?"

"Negative."

"Well, he's a fair man."

"John, what the Grand Panjandrums are thinking is the least of your worries. Bluto will be catching a plane out of Dulles in a couple of hours, along with some bloodhounds. They're going to be looking for you. Every station is alerted. By this time tomorrow you are going to be much in demand—and we're not talking border guards and cops on the beat. This is a major flap, and the Agency is putting out their best to find you. You're going to have to be careful."

"Kevin, I'm always careful." Paine paused a moment. "Look, telling me what you have so far, well, you've already done enough to warrant dismissal . . ."

Cunningham laughed again. "Hell, just taking this phone call was enough to warrant dismissal. They've asked me to report any contacts. I guess they figured you would get in touch eventually."

"Well, now that you've crossed the line, I'm going to ask you to go a little further. Feel free to refuse."

"I don't like the sound of this."

"You won't. I need to know what, if anything, we've got planned for Europe. I'm looking for a clean operation."

Cunningham sounded wary. "John," he said soberly, "are you asking me to reveal details of a running plan? Something you're not in on? Are you crazy?"

Paine waited a few long seconds before replying. "No, Kevin, I'm not crazy. I'm desperate."

"What do you need to know? And why?"

"I have a theory..."

"Oh God, I hate your theories."

"Then you're really going to hate this one."

"I can't wait."

"I think there's a mole at Langley. There's a double at the top or close to it, and for some reason, he's afraid of me. I know something that can blow his cover."

"What?"

"I don't know yet."

"You're crazy."

"Maybe. But Kevin, someone keeps on trying to kill me, set me up, and/or generally make my life difficult. Christ, the other day someone tried to kill me with a saxophone."

In spite of himself and the seriousness of the situation, Cunningham laughed. "Never heard of that before. Tell me, did he try to play you to death—you know, 'Take the A Train' over and over again until you dropped—or did he just try to hit you with it?"

"He tried to hit me with it."

"I'll have to pass that on to technical. Coulda been worse, coulda been a sousaphone. Now, that'd *hurt*."

"Funny, Cunningham. Do we have something going down in Europe, something I can use?"

"I had hoped you had forgotten."

"I haven't."

Cunningham took a deep breath. "I don't know where you are, but can you get to Lugano, in Switzerland?"

"Yes."

"There's a drop there, scheduled for the fifteenth of this month. Five hundred thousand dollars going to your friends and mine the Ukrainians. The Agency is funneling money into the Soviet republics to pay for the independence movements. Two of them are meeting one of ours. A simple exchange."

"Where?"

"On a lake steamer."

"When?"

Paine couldn't see Cunningham shrug. "When they can. I don't know much more than that."

"It'll have to do."

"John, what the hell are you up to? Just what are you planning?"

"I'm planning to clear my name, Kevin. That's all."

"Christ, be careful."

"I told you, I'm always careful."

"Look, I'm sure that my phone is going to be having a little trouble. I have a feeling that someone is going to show up in a clean, shiny phone company uniform and—"

"Yeah. You remember the fallback plan?"

"The one you christened 'Hey Jude'?"

"That's the one. We'll use that from now on."

"Roger that."

"Take care, Kevin. Watch your ass."

"I can't, John. I'm always sitting down." Cunningham replaced the phone and wheeled himself out of the booth. He had been watching the parking lot throughout his conversation with Paine. Apart from what appeared to be normal traffic for a twenty-four-hour supermarket, no cars had pulled into the lot, and Cunningham felt reasonably secure. Secure, that is, that he had made it into the lot undetected and that he would be able to get out and home safely. As he drove away from the supermarket, however, he couldn't shake a single, unsettling thought: he had revealed an Agency secret to John Paine, and in doing so, Kevin Cunningham had committed a crime: treason.

16

Not even Charlie Sullivan liked Bluto. He and Grove had trailed out to the airport to meet Bluto and his team, standing on the tarmac waiting for an Agency plane to taxi in, as if the Internal Security man were a visiting dignitary.

"Why the hell didn't we have the Marine band out here?" grumbled Sullivan. "And we should have gotten Kohl to show up too, maybe an honor guard. Jesus, Sam, this is ridiculous, the number one and two of Berlin station out here to meet a jerk like Bluto. The whole of Berlin—both sides—is going to know he's here—"

"They'd know anyway," said Grove.

"—and that means our friends and the other side are going to figure out that something's up."

"They figured that already."

"You know what I mean. Why the hell couldn't we be a little more discreet about this bullshit?"

"We were ordered to meet him. We meet him," said Grove simply.

The jet engine's scream died down a little, and the panel door folded in on itself and popped open. Bill "Bluto" Mitchell appeared in the doorway, waiting impatiently for the stairway to be rolled into place. For a moment it looked as if he couldn't be bothered waiting for the stairs, and Grove thought he was going to jump the eight or ten feet to the tarmac.

He strode down onto the hardstand, two young men following him. They were expressionless and wore very dark glasses. They looked to Grove and Sullivan like secret service men. They weren't.

"I don't know if you know my team, Sam," said Bluto, shouting over the sound of the jet engines.

"I don't," said Grove.

"Me neither," said Sullivan.

"Buck," said Bluto, jerking a thumb at one of the serious young men, "Hank."

Neither Buck nor Hank said anything as they slipped into the front seats of the Embassy Cadillac limousine that had pulled up. Grove settled himself in the plush interior and looked past Bluto to the square heads of Buck and Hank, and the thick necks. Christ, he thought, they weren't *too* obvious.

Bluto was forced to take one of the jump seats, and he squeezed his bulk onto it, his knees almost in his face. Sullivan looked out the window, ignoring the beefy enforcer, hoping that if he didn't acknowledge him, he might vanish.

"So," said Bluto, "what you got for me?"

Grove sighed. "Paine's alias was James Deveraux. We gave it to him. He cashed five grand into deutsch marks at the airport in Hannover. Then he ditched his car in Vienna..."

"Where he greased the priest."

"Where Father Beck was murdered," said Sullivan, still looking out the window.

"Yeah, yeah."

"As John Paine, he crossed into Italy."

"Shit. Italy. I fuckin' hate Italy. All those fuckin' Italians."

"John Paine stayed in a hotel in Venice," continued Grove. "He checked out after one night. Hasn't been heard from since."

"That's it?"

Sullivan shrugged. "That's it."

"Then what the fuck are we doing here? We should be in Italy, for Christ's sake."

"We were sort of wondering ourselves, Bill," said Grove.

"Shit. Stop the car."

Grove spoke into the intercom, and the big limo stopped on the tarmac just in front of the private arrivals terminal. Bluto banged on the glass, and the partition slid down.

"Buck, Hank. Go get the plane gassed up, and have the pilot file a flight plan for Venice." The two men nodded and jumped out of the car.

"Sam, can you get some local Eyetie spook to

meet us at the airport in Venice, someone who can help? Have him meet us with a car and take us into town so we can talk to the people at the hotel Paine stayed at. We'll have to work from there."

"A car?" said Sullivan archly.

"Yeah. You know, a car: four tires, seats, an engine, you know, Sully. Like a Buick or something." Bluto thought he was being funny and had a feeling that Sullivan had an aversion to being called Sully.

"Bill," said Sullivan, "there are no cars in Venice. The streets are filled with water, remember?"

"Fuck," said Bluto.

"I'll have someone meet you with a boat," said Grove soothingly. "You'll like Venice, Bill. It's a very pretty place."

"Who gives a fuck?" said Bluto.

The next forty-five minutes were like the arrival scene played in reverse. The plane reappeared; Grove and Sullivan stood in front of it with Bluto, Hank, and Buck while the IS men fumed waiting for the stairs to be wheeled into position. Finally they came; the three men bounded up the steps, waved to Grove and Sullivan, and slammed the door. The plane taxied away.

"Which one was Buck and which one was Hank?" asked Grove.

* * *

A major in the DIGOS, the Italian counter-intelligence service, met the searchers from the CIA at the Venice airport. He picked Bluto out of the crowd immediately and stepped forward to greet him.

"I am Scarfiotti, Mr. Mitchell. Aldo Scarfiotti."

"I'm Mitchell," said Bluto, "Hank and Buck."

Hank and Buck nodded and continued to chew their gum.

"I have a boat waiting." A naval rating stood of the foredeck of a powerful speedboat, keeping the ship alongside the dock with a boat hook. Within a few minutes the minimal luggage had been taken aboard, and the ship rocketed out across the Venetian lagoon toward the heart of the city. The skipper maneuvered through the narrow canals as if he were behind the wheel of a sports car, scarcely glancing at the canal traffic. The beauty of the scene was lost on Bluto and his team. Buck and Hank peered through the cabin windows at the pedestrians on the bridges and narrow paths as if hoping to catch a glimpse of Paine.

The hotel Paine had occupied was one of the better ones and boasted a canal-side entrance. The skipper of the speedboat pulled up to the gate of the hotel like a cab driver stopping to drop a fare. The hotel manager had been alerted to the arrival of these unorthodox guests and he stood nervously at the pier.

"Any of my staff who had the slightest contact

with this Paine," he said, ushering his visitors into his office, "are at your service."

"'Preciate it," said Bluto, looking around the office suspiciously as if it might be bugged.

"They are waiting in the staff lounge, but you are welcome to use my office for your—er—interrogations."

"Good. They speak English?"

"Most of them," said the manager.

"I will translate," offered Scarfiotti.

"Fine. Start sending them in."

Only four staff members had any contact with John Paine, and not one of them could offer any information of importance. The receptionist who checked him remembered that he was quiet and made no special requests for his room.

"People are very demanding," he explained. "They must have a canal view, a king-size bed, a quiet room, a view of San Marco. Sir, we don't even face San Marco, I say, but it makes no difference. This one, the man you look for, he asked for nothing; that alone is why I remember him."

"He didn't meet anybody, make any phone calls?"

"No, sir."

"Nothing strange about him?"

"Nothing, sir. He paid his bill in advance—"

"How?"

"In cash. In lire. I do remember thinking that he was not like a man on holiday."

"You can say that again," growled Bluto.

Paine's registration card gave his home address as New York City and stated that his next destination was Florence.

"That's sure to be phony," said Bluto. "Buck, get on to Rome and see if what's his name—Cannon—can get some people looking in Florence for him. It's bound to be a wild-goose chase, but what the hell, might as well check it out."

"Yessir," said Buck. He looked suspiciously at the hotel manager and the man from Italian counterintelligence. "Should I make the call in here?"

"Please," said the hotel manager. "If you prefer, you may use the phone on the desk of my secretary."

"Better," said Buck.

The porter who carried Paine's bags, the chambermaid who cleaned his room, and the morning concierge who checked him out had nothing to add to the scant details of the portrait of Paine's stay in Venice. Bluto had to think.

He and his two henchmen marched out of the hotel, striding through the narrow streets and up and down the steep bridges, never looking at the beauty of the city around them.

"So what the fuck was he doing here?" said Bluto aloud. The three men strode three abreast down the narrow *calli*, a wall of business-suited beef which filled the street. Pedestrians had to shrink against the walls to let them pass.

"Maybe he was making contact with the KGB," said Hank, who did not comprehend the concept of innocent until proven guilty.

"That would be risky," said Buck, who wasn't as dumb as he looked.

"How's that?"

"Look at this city, sir. It's an island. He couldn't have risked getting bottled up here. We could isolate it at any time. Seal the bridge which links it with the mainland and patrol the bay, and he'd be caught like a rat in a trap."

They were standing at the peak of one of the bridges. Bluto surveyed the maze of narrow streets and canals stretched in front of him. "Some trap. You could hide forever in this fuckin' town."

"I don't think forever, sir," said Buck.

Bluto shrugged. "You could be right. If he wasn't here to make contact, then what was he here for?"

Hank and Buck shook their heads.

Then Bluto realized they were lost. "Fuckit."

The American consul in Venice was not used to three CIA men dropping in on him, and unlike his counterpart in Hanover, he was not thrilled by the honor.

"You must understand, gentlemen, this is a very small State Department post. Mostly we deal with cultural matters like the Venice *Biennale*, which I'm sure you've heard about. Art exchanges, that sort of thing. I spend more time corresponding with museum directors than I do with Foggy Bottom."

Bluto grunted. "Art shows."

"That is correct. Beyond that, there are some visas to be processed, a little trade, and, of course, replacing the documents of American tourists unlucky enough to lose their wallets or their purses."

"That happen a lot?"

"Goodness, yes. Theft and just plain careless-ness."

Careless, thought Bluto, was one thing Paine was not. "Now what?" He looked to Buck and Hank.

Both men shrugged. They knew what had to happen next, and neither of them were happy about it. They couldn't do a damn thing until Paine made his next move. Right now he con-trolled the board.

17

By all rights, Lugano, in the southern part, the Italian part, of Switzerland, should be one of the ideal cities in Europe. It should combine Swiss efficiency with Italian food and general happiness. It does not. The city is beautifully situated on Lake Lugano, with the picture book splendor of the Alps rising behind it. It is, like all cities in Switzerland, clean and well run. The people speak Italian, but they are not Italian. They are Swiss: sober, quiet, dull, hardworking; they are also lousy cooks.

John Paine was not a finicky eater, but he pushed away in disgust the plate of lasagna that he had been served in one of the lakeside restaurants. It was burnt on the outside, frozen in the middle, and tasted like cardboard.

Still, he wasn't in Lugano to eat. He picked up the Canon 35-millimeter camera mounted with a 120-millimeter long-focus zoom lens he had bought himself that morning and swept the lake, focusing in close on the steamer *Anna-Luisa* that was cruising the placid blue waters, taking tourists on a little water jaunt. Paine had no intention of photographing anything, but a camera with an ordinary long lens was far less conspicuous than a pair of binoculars. A man sitting at a table by the water's edge with a camera was a tourist looking for a nice shot to show the folks back home. A lone man with a pair of high-powered field glasses was a spy.

Identifying the CIA contact who was going to make the drop in Lugano was easier than he expected. He knew the man, by sight anyway. His name was Harvey MacIntosh, an old European war-horse of the Sam Grove era. He had never been a spectacular agent, and rumor had it that he went through a bad bout with the bottle. Still, here he was still in the field, working with the trust of his superiors, even if it was just doing a little bullshit courier work. Paine could see in an instant why MacIntosh's career had not been a great one. He had arrived at the gangplank of the *Anna-Luisa* in a Mercedes cab, dressed in a suit and carrying a briefcase, as if he were an insurance agent who wanted to talk a little business on a Swiss lake steamer. He didn't actually stand out—mainly because people never really noticed other people, Paine had found—but he didn't blend in either.

The two Ukrainians had been far more professional, even though they weren't operatives in the true sense of the word; Paine had not been able to make them among the families and couples who marched on to the trim little ship.

Paine had decided that he would not travel on the steamer once he discovered that it was a cruise to nowhere. It didn't call at any of the ports that dotted the lakeshore. It simply sailed around for an hour or two, then returned. If he had gone aboard, there was the chance that MacIntosh would have recognized him. Better to keep to a discreet distance on land. He would pick up the trail when the ship returned to its berth. In the meantime, he kept watch on the vessel and ignored his lasagna.

His waiter, who was Italian from Italy—the Swiss imported Italians to do what they considered to be menial jobs—could see that Paine didn't much care for the cuisine.

"No like?" he asked, looking sadly at the food and then toward the mountains. On the other side of them lay Italy.

Paine smiled. "Merda," he said.

The Italian brightened slightly. "Of course it's shit," he replied in Italian. "The cook is from Turkey! A Turkish cook in Switzerland. Can you think of anything worse?"

"No," Paine agreed.

The waiter picked up his plate. "Eh," he said. "Maybe you want something else. This is a very expensive restaurant, you know. You have to pay just to put your ass in the seat."

"Bring me some wine," said Paine. "And some fruit."

The waiter nodded approvingly. "Much better. Both are from Italia."

The *Anna-Luisa* was nosing back toward Lugano as he finished his wine, a mere quarter liter. It was time for a little action. He paid the bill, tipped the waiter heavily, then walked to his rented BMW. He started the powerful engine and drove the lakeside road to the steamer slip.

A crowd of tourists waiting to board the ship congregated at the base of the gangplank waiting for the newly returned passengers to disembark. Paine mingled with them, holding his camera at his side as if it were a weapon. He spotted MacIntosh—no briefcase—in one of the companionways and fixed him in his lens. The man was walking with the exaggerated care of a drunk, threading his way through the crowd making for the gangway. At the top of the steep stairway he tottered for a moment as the crowd seemed to surge forward—very un-Swiss—like a bunch of commuters pushing to get on a subway train. Paine just had time to register the glazed look in MacIntosh's eyes in the camera lens before the spy tumbled down the gangway.

There was a scream from the crowd as MacIntosh thumped down the steps, his bald head cracking painfully on the iron railing. It seemed to take forever for MacIntosh to stop, his bulk wedged two-thirds of the way down the steps. Blood gushed from a cut in his scalp, and his eyes were now wide and staring.

"*Il est mort!*" shouted a French tourist.

A ship's officer dressed in whites as spit-and-polish as if he manned the bridge of a carrier appeared and shouted something in Switze-deutsch to some worried-looking crewmen. A very non-Swiss confusion reigned for a few minutes: a policeman appeared and shooed away the crowd waiting to board the vessel, an ambulance pulled up, and MacIntosh was hustled away. The remaining passengers on board the ship were allowed off, and that was what Paine was waiting for.

The officious cop was still trying to get him to clear the scene when two young men came off the ship. They were the kind of tourists one sees all over Europe in high season. They were slovenly dressed in T-shirts and baggy shorts, no socks, and sneakers. One carried a guitar case, a common enough piece of luggage for the backpack set—except Paine noticed that it was the only bag carried off the ship large enough to contain half a million dollars cash.

The policeman finally succeeded in getting Paine away from the berth. He trailed the two young tourists a block or two inland from the lakeshore and knew, suddenly, that he was following the right people. The two kids did something out of character for their type: they hailed a taxi. Kids traveling through Europe on the cheap didn't take taxis, particularly Swiss taxis, which were hideously expensive.

He waited until the taxi had pulled away from the rank, then took the one behind it.

"Where is that cab going?" he asked the driver.

"I don't know."

"Were there two kids in it, one with a guitar case?"

The driver half turned in his seat to get a look at Paine. "Yes; what of it?"

Paine slapped his knee. "I knew it! I think one of them is my nephew. Follow them. My sister told me that he was going to be in Switzerland. How do you like that, running into him like that."

The cab driver really didn't care. He slapped on the meter and pulled into traffic, orderly Swiss traffic, which meant they had to keep their place in line three or four cars behind.

"Can't you go faster?" asked Paine, hoping he sounded like a doting uncle.

"No," said the driver, "it is forbidden."

"Damn," said Paine. But that was fine with him; a few car lengths back was just where he wanted to be.

They crossed a couple of miles of the pretty city, the driver shadowing the car better than he knew. After a few minutes; the driver spoke.

"I know where they're going."

"Where?"

"The youth hostel near the train station. Or

maybe the station itself, but I think the hostel. Those are the only two things on this side of the city that a foreigner would go to."

The lead car slowed, as if it had heard Paine's driver, and pulled up in front of the redbrick building that had a sign on its facade proclaiming in a dozen languages that it was the home for youth in Lugano. The two young men paid off the cab.

"Damn," said Paine. "That's not Charlie."

The cab driver shrugged. "You want me to stop?"

"At the end of the block."

The cab pulled over. "Twenty-one francs." Paine paid and waited until the car was lost in traffic, crossed the street, and entered a café, ordering a cup of coffee, which he carried to a table in the window looking out toward the hostel. The coffee bar plainly catered to the residents of the youth center: Paine was the oldest person in the room and the best-dressed, although he wore nothing more flashy than khaki pants, an old blue oxford-cloth shirt, and loafers. A boy with a straggly Vandyke beard tried to bum some money off him in half a dozen languages, not one of which Paine claimed to know. Music poured from some speakers, a Swiss rock star singing a song in German about how the state should be turned into cucumber salad; that was about as radical as Switzerland got.

Paine sat in these uncomfortable and dispiriting surroundings for ten or fifteen minutes.

Then the two tourists appeared, towering back-packs strapped to their backs—and one still carried a guitar case.

No taxis this time; the two kids started out on foot toward the train station. Paine drained his coffee and followed.

The train station looked as if it had been stolen from a child's train set and enlarged. It was pretty, and Swiss as only Swiss railway stations could be, with stationmasters patrolling the platforms as if they were prison guards. The two boys stood in line at the ticket window, Paine directly behind them, hoping he would overhear their destination. As they neared the ticket clerk, it became obvious that he wouldn't have to: as soon as a passenger announced his destination, the clerk pressed a button and the information appeared on a TV screen facing the traveler: place, time of departure, track number, and price. The two bought one-way second-class tickets to Zurich. Paine did the same.

The midafternoon train to Zurich wasn't crowded, so the two young men looked surprised, then suspicious, when Paine slid open the door of their compartment. The train had just pulled out of Lugano, picking up speed. The two shifted in their seats when Paine came in. Everyone knew that if you could have a compartment to yourself, you took it—and there were plenty of empty compartments on the train.

Paine dropped into a seat and opened the *In-*

ternational Herald Tribune he had bought at the station newstand. The two young travelers were quiet a moment.

Then one said: "What do you think?" He was speaking in German, Prussian German: East German German.

There was a long silence. "Just some American."

"No luggage."

They kept their voices low and conversational. If you didn't speak the language, then you would have thought they were wondering what time the train would arrive in Zurich.

"Coincidence?"

There's no such thing, thought Paine.

There was a long silence. Then: "Probably."

The compartment door swept open. *"Fichen, billets, biglietti*, tickets," said the conductor. Paine handed his over, as did the boys. The conductor studied them for a moment, satisfying himself that they weren't forgeries, then punched them full of holes.

"Danke, merci, grazie, thank you." He slid the door shut. Paine folded his paper and smiled at the two young men.

"So where are you fellas headed?"

The two young men looked at each other, then at Paine, and shrugged.

"Don't speak English? *Ingliss?*"

The two men shrugged again and smirked at each other.

Paine looked out the window at the bright

Swiss sunlight. "Say, you don't think it will rain, do you? You don't suppose I should have brought along a *mackintosh?*"

The two men froze; Paine's eyes turned cold and he snapped the lock shut on the door and pulled down the shades. "Let's talk," he said in German.

Both young men looked at the luggage racks; Paine could almost see their eyes burrowing into the backpacks to the guns that he was now sure were hidden there.

"What do you want?"

"I want to know who you are."

"We are tourists."

"No you're not."

"Sir, I do not like your tone of voice."

"My God," said Paine, shaking his head, "the KGB is working with children now."

One of them did his best to laugh. "The KGB!"

Paine shrugged. "KGB, GRU, maybe Spetznaz."

Both young men were deathly pale under their Guns 'n Roses T-shirts. Paine guessed it was their first time out: a simple mission to scam the CIA out of a bundle of money and to knock off a drunk operative from the Agency, an old man who should have been put out to grass years ago.

"Sir, I wish to call the conductor."

Paine settled back in his seat. "Fine. But how will you explain the weapons in your packs? The Swiss are very touchy about foreign tourists running around their country with guns."

"We have no guns."

Paine smiled again. "I guess I made a mistake." He stood up. "Just a couple of students wandering around Europe, huh? Then why don't you play me a tune on your guitar?" As soon as Paine touched the guitar case, things started to happen very quickly. Both young men jumped to their feet, almost colliding with each other in the confined space. Paine hooked his hands over the luggage rack and hefted himself off the ground, landing one of his feet neatly in the throat of one of the men. With the other he was not so lucky: he ducked the kick and came at Paine, throwing him off balance with a sharp punch to the body. Paine felt the force of the blow slam into his ribs and he staggered back against the wall of the coach. The kid was unpolished, but he was strong.

The one who had his windpipe closed with the sharp spear kick was lying against the vinyl banquette of the carriage, gagging and wretching. The other, though, was pressing his advantage. He shouted something in German and struck again; Paine slipped under the punch and came up with both elbows out, sharp as porcupine quills—or so they seemed when they slammed into each eye of the kid, the round of the elbow fitting neatly into each socket. He screamed and dropped to his knees, tearing at his eyes, which bled through his bruised lids.

Paine wasn't finished. He cracked his heel

against the back of the boy's head, dropping him flat to the ground like a rug. Straining to breathe, the other one just held his throat and stared at Paine with frightened eyes.

Paine rested his foot on the throat of the fallen one, ready to close his windpipe if trouble arose in that quarter.

"Okay, sonny, what's going on here?"

"I won't answer you," shrieked the kid.

"You killed MacIntosh."

"You can prove nothing!"

Paine grabbed him by his T-shirt and slammed him back against the wall of the carriage. He stared into his eyes. "I don't have to prove anything."

"But—"

There was a groan from the prostrate form at Paine's feet. Without looking down, he increased the pressure on the kid's throat.

"Help," he hacked.

Paine pressed down harder. "Shuttup."

"Now, listen to me, both of you. You will tell me who sent you, for what purpose, and what your next move is supposed to be. Or—" Paine sounded quite reasonable "—I will kill you."

The boy still sitting on the upholstered bench shrugged. "You, them, what difference does it make?"

"Who are you?"

"We are soldiers."

"Shuttup!" hissed the one on the floor.

"Whose soldiers?"

"Of the Democratic Republic of Germany."

"Rank?"

"Sergeant."

"Him?" said Paine, glancing down.

"Also."

"Your mission?"

"To meet the American..."

"And?"

"Take the money..."

"And?"

Neither boy spoke.

"*And?*" demanded Paine.

"Kill him."

"Why?"

"I don't know."

Paine wanted to know more, but the train was slowing down, coming into the first station after Lugano. In a moment they would pull into the station, and the scene in the car would be clearly visible from the platform. Even assuming no one bothered to look in, people would be moving along the corridor of the train; they would try the door. It was time to go.

He hauled the kid on the floor to his feet and threw him down next to his companion. He stripped off their belts and bound them as securely as he could. It wasn't satisfactory, but he hoped that he would gain enough time to get off the train and make his getaway. He snapped open the guitar case: piles of dollars seemed to wink back at him. He searched through their backpacks as quickly as he could, discovered two West German passports, and pocketed them. He also took the two Browning nine-millimeter handguns with thirteen-shot clips, each filled with the full complement of bullets. He slipped them into the guitar case.

The train was crawling now. "I just want to know, how did you kill MacIntosh?"

"I don't have to tell you anything."

"That's not very grateful. I could kill you now."

"We'll die anyway," said one of the young men. Suddenly, without warning, he began to cry.

"Defect," said Paine.

"They'll catch us in Zurich."

"Don't go to Zurich."

"Where can we go?" he said through his tears. "No money, no passports . . ."

"I'll give you your passports back and some money; just tell me how you killed MacIntosh?"

"How can we trust you?"

"You can't." Paine glanced out the window. The suburbs of a Swiss town were slowly crawling by. "I'd guess that we have about three minutes before we reach the station. I'll be gone in about thirty seconds. I'd say you have no choice, children."

The young soldiers exchanged glances. "We were given a drug called Athenenmine. They said it would mix with the alcohol in his drink and would be undetectable. When he fell down the gangway, he was supposed to do enough damage to kill himself, or look like he had died in the fall, you know."

"I've never heard of that stuff."

"Neither have we. We're soldiers, not chemists."

"I have a feeling you'd make better chemists," said Paine, heading for the door, hefting the guitar case.

"Wait!" shrieked one. "Where are you going?"

"I'm getting out of here."

"But, but . . ."

"But what?"

"The passports! The money!"

Paine shrugged. "You should learn not to be so trusting." He slid open the door and then closed it with a click.

He dropped off the train before the carriage stopped moving. There was silence from the compartment he had shared with the two soldiers: he could imagine that they were lying there trussed, trying to decided what to do next. Should they raise the roof and claim they had been robbed? Should they try and work themselves free and strike out on their own? Either way, they were still thinking about it when Paine caught a country bus that took him back to Lugano.

18

Paine arrived back in Lugano late in the afternoon and went shopping. He found a stationery
shop and bought a couple of heavy mailing en-
velopes, some brown paper, Scotch tape, and
string.

He returned to his hotel, helped himself to a
beer from the little refrigerator in the corner,
and popped it open, drinking while he took the
money from the guitar case, making sure as he
did so that he got his fingerprints all over the
bills. On a piece of Hotel du Lac writing paper,
he wrote a simple sentence: "We have a problem."

Then he bound the money in the brown paper,
securing the package firmly with tape and
string. On that package he wrote: "DCI
ONLY"—knowing as he did so that his request
would not be honored—and stuffed the whole
thing into one envelope, then another. On that
he wrote the address of a CIA "cold" address in

Alexandria, Virginia. He tucked the package under his arm, and fifteen minutes later he consigned his package of "documents"—that's what he declared the money to be on the customs forms—to the hands of the DHL international messenger service. An hour later he turned in his car at the rental agency and, as Mervyn Holst, caught a train for France.

"'We have a problem,'" quoted the DCI. "That, gentlemen, is something of an understatement."

Langley was in an uproar. Another agent had died; the operation to deliver the money into friendly Russian hands had been a fiasco. Paine had come out of nowhere and . . . and what? Returned the money.

"Now, why the hell would he do that?" wondered Endicott.

None of them—not Weinberg or Berghold or the DCI himself—had any idea. Cunningham stared at the pad of blank paper on the conference table.

"Well," said Berghold, head of Internal Security, trying to look on the bright side, "at least we know where he is, or rather, was."

"How the hell did he know to go to Lugano in the first place?" demanded Weinberg.

"Maybe he was tipped off by Moscow and they sent him in to do the dirty work." Endicott produced a pipe and started the complicated process of lighting up.

"And return the money?" countered Berghold. "That's just a ruse."

"Hell of a ruse," said the Director of Central Intelligence. "Kevin, you haven't been in touch with him, have you?"

Cunningham looked his superior in the eye. "No, sir."

"You haven't," said Weinberg. "You're sure?"

All eyes were on Cunningham. "I have a feeling I would remember if I had, Tom."

"You wouldn't have any trouble with a lie detector test, then, would you?"

"No, Tom, I wouldn't."

"I don't think we've come to that point yet," said Endicott nervously. The Paine thing was upsetting, but not nearly as upsetting as the thought of a traitor on the European desk—so close to Endicott's retirement.

"Why not? I think we should all be clear in our own minds that Kevin is being straight with us."

"And what makes you think I'm not, Tom?" said Cunningham, doing his best to keep his voice even.

"Come on, Kevin. If anyone in this room is rooting for Paine, it's you. Are you sure that you haven't been helping him out? I'm not suggesting that you're working for the other side, nothing like that. It's just that I think you might have let your friendship with Paine warp your judgment."

"I'm ready for a polygraph any time you care to set one up."

Berghold smiled behind his hand. Weinberg looked to the DCI. "You see, sir, if Kevin himself has no objections, then I think we should proceed."

"I don't think that will be necessary," said Berghold.

"Why the hell not, Mark? You're the head of IS. Your guys are running around giving polygraphs to every schmuck who drives by on the Beltway."

"Yes," said Berghold slowly, "but in this case..."

"Above all in this case."

Cunningham watched the two men sparring, turning his head as if watching a tennis match.

"Kevin," said Berghold, "correct me if I'm wrong—and I don't wish to bring up a painful subject here—but your injuries..."

"Yes, Mark?"

"I'd guess there was pretty extensive damage to the spine, is there not?"

"Very extensive," said Cunningham, smiling slightly. Berghold knew.

"Tom, I'm not going to give you a long lecture on how a polygraph machine works, but let me just tell you that Kevin, if he were hooked up to one, would read out like a neon sign on the fritz. Sorry, Kevin, it's not a very elegant metaphor."

"But apt."

"You mean that Kevin wouldn't give a reading because of his, his, injuries."

"That's about it."

"Son of a bitch," said Weinberg. Suddenly he didn't think hiring the handicapped was such a great idea. When he became DCI someday, he'd change that.

Bluto and his team touched down in Lugano the morning after Paine left. The three men were furious with themselves and furious at Paine. There seemed to be no way of catching him—they were sure that Lugano would yield as few clues as Venice. They were, however, surprised by Paine's change of identity.

"Who the fuck is Mervyn Holst?" demanded Bluto when shown Paine's registration papers. "Is that an Agency ID?"

"I'll check," said Buck, reaching for one of the phones in the manager's office.

"He must have ditched that identity by now," observed Hank.

"I fuckin' know that. Just add it to the list of aliases and get the rest looking for Paine aka Holst. Shit."

Along with looking for Paine, Langley had asked Mitchell to identify the body of MacIntosh in the Lugano municipal mortuary. It was not a job Bluto had relished, not because it made him queasy, but because it detracted from his status and subtracted time from his search.

However, when the sheet was pulled back,

uncovering MacIntosh's deathly pale face, the cut on his scalp neatly stitched, Mitchell felt a stab of emotion.

"Mac MacIntosh was a friend of mine," he said to Buck and Hank. "I swear to you boys, I'm gonna get that fuckin' Paine and nail his ass good." Buck and Hank nodded ominously. Bluto pulled the sheet back over MacIntosh's face. "Mac was a great guy. One of my best friends," he said, although in truth, he had only known the dead man slightly.

It was Hank who noticed the article on the second page of the *International Herald Tribune*. They had broken for lunch, and the young man was paging through the newspaper because no one felt much like talking.

"Hey, look at this." He shoved the paper under Bluto's nose.

The headline read: "Swiss Police Puzzled: Double Slaying on Train."

" 'Two German tourists were murdered yesterday while on a train journey from Lugano to Zurich, Swiss police officials report. The two men, aged twenty-one and twenty-two, were found at four-fifteen yesterday afternoon in their second-class compartment. Both had been shot in the head with a high-caliber hand gun. Both had been shot at close range. Their identities are being withheld pending the notification of their families. A spokesman for the Swiss railways, Hans Huffheinz, expressed concern and shock, adding, "This is not a normal occurrence on the Swiss rail system."'"

Bluto put down the paper. "Pass the word," he said grimly. "He's armed."

Hundreds of miles to the south, in Nice, on the French Riviera, Paine sat in a café on the Boulevard Austerlitz and read the same story. His blood chilled: he was being followed, shadowed by someone who was watching his every move. Each time Paine struck, the shadow was right behind him: first Father Beck, now the two kids on the train.

Paine stood up and tossed away the paper. It was time to disappear.

Merv Holst lay on the warm, dark sands of the island of Lipari off the coast of Sicily. It was the last day of his summer vacation, and he lay with his eyes closed, soaking up the warm sun, in his mind adding up the credit card receipts he could remember. Not including airfare, the two weeks had cost him something on the order of three thousand bucks. Still, it had been worth it. His daughter, Courtney, and her friend Kimberly had had a great time, finishing up here in these great islands, one of which even had a volcano. It was sort of like being in Hawaii.

The two girls were lying by his side baking in the sun, desperate to get their last bit of tanning done.

Overall, thought Holst, it had been one hell

of a vacation. Something Courtney's mother was going to have to work hard to top. What the hell was three grand compared to that?

"Holst!" shouted someone.

Merv opened his eyes and then sat up, stunned. Four men, all dressed in suits, were standing over him. They all had guns pointed at him. A cordon of blue-uniformed Italian police cut him off from the rest of the beach. They, alarmingly, held submachine guns.

"Jesus Christ!" screeched Holst.

"Daddy!" yelled Courtney.

"One move and you're a dead motherfucker," said a man from the CIA.

19

Someone once called Monte Carlo "a sunny place for shady people." While the world at large knew the tiny principality on the French Riviera as a playground for the superrich, home to fabulously luxurious hotels and the famous casino, it was better known in some quarters as a place where people asked no questions about sudden affluence. One's money could have come from some dubious stock deals or simple outright theft; it didn't matter, as long as you had money, lots of it. The Monte Carlo police were famous for their zeal in protecting the very rich; be they old rich or new rich, rich was rich. A Monte Carlo matron once observed: "They might be the Gestapo, but they're *our* Gestapo."

Where there is money, there are people like Rocque. He didn't live in Monte Carlo—he wasn't rich enough—but in Cap d'Ail, the poor back alley yard of the city, a rocky, beachless, yachtless promontory near Monte Carlo but actually located in France. The rich in Monte Carlo needed servants, hotel chambermaids, drivers, street sweepers, and garbage men; they needed them close at hand but not, heaven knows, in the same city. Cap d'Ail didn't look like a slum—that would have spoiled the view—but there was nothing terribly rich about it either.

Rocque was a servant of sorts. He provided women to the men, boys to the women, boys to the boys. If you needed a gun or someone who knew how to use one, then Rocque could fix you up. If you needed incriminating pictures of your husband frolicking on a yacht off the Cote d'Azur, then Rocque would hire the speedboat and get the photographer. All you needed was money.

He had not seen Paine for years but was not surprised to see him when Paine took a chair across from his at a small café in Cap d'Ail.

"Ah," said Rocque, "the mysterious Mr. Paine. Many people are looking for you, you know." Rocque was a broad-shouldered man, perpetually tanned. He wore glasses and looked myopic when he took them off. He would have passed in any crowd.

"I had a feeling."

"And why have you come to see me, Mr. Paine?"

"For a pastis and a chat."

Rocque shouted to the barman, who brought two pastis. He waited until Paine had finished his before he spoke. "Now you have had your drink, what would you like to chat about?"

"Boats," said Paine.

"Ah. You wish to buy a boat."

"I'm not rich enough to buy a boat, Monsieur Rocque."

Rocque looked sad. "That is a very great pity. I know of some very nice boats for sale. There are many, more than you would think. There are hard times on the Riviera, you know. The oil glut, that stupid stock market crash..."

"Hard times on the Riviera," said Paine. "I don't believe it."

"Relative to other places, you understand."

"Of course."

"So, Mr. Paine, what would you like to say about boats?"

"I'd like to say that I'm looking for a boat that I can join as a member of the crew."

"Ah, you don't want a boat, Mr. Paine. You want a *job*. Maybe the Loews Hotel needs some dishwashers."

"I need a job on a boat."

"I see. This, of course, has something to do with the people who are looking for you, does it not?"

"It does."

Rocque thought for a moment. There was no point in turning Paine in. Intelligence agencies did not pay rewards, not to informers at least, and besides, he liked Paine and felt a certain affinity with anyone on the run from the law.

"Yes, I know of a boat which requires a crew member. Can you be a waiter?"

"I was thinking more of a deckhand."

"I know a boat looking for a cabin steward. That is the only thing going at the moment." Rocque smiled. The idea of the feared CIA man in a steward's mess jacket handing around hot hors d'oeuvres appealed to him.

"Then I suppose I must take it. What is the ship?"

"It is a yacht, a big one, under charter to an American, a film producer. It is lying in Monte Carlo now and is headed out for—" Rocque shrugged "—wherever the very rich people on board care to go. I don't know. Sardegna, perhaps, Corsica, Italy, Greece, Turkey. They have no schedule. They are *very* rich."

"What do I have to do?"

"*Tiens*," said Rocque, looking perplexed. "You probably do not have any papers. Everything requires papers, you know."

"I have a wallet full of papers."

"What kind?"

"Deutsch marks."

"Now, those, Mr. Paine, are very good papers. I'm glad to see that some Americans, at least, have discovered that doors do not pop open at the mere sight of dollars. Deutsch marks are good. Swiss francs are better." Rocque was a true connoisseur of currency.

"I would like five thousand marks, and in return I will see that you have all the papers you need and an ironclad introduction to the captain of the *Sea Dawn*—that is the ship."

"And a passport."

"Eight thousand deutsch marks."

"Seven thousand."

"No, eight," said Rocque firmly.

Paine shrugged. "Fine."

"Of course it is fine; it is a bargain."

Rocque moved quickly. By eight o'clock that night Paine had acquired a set of seaman's papers, attesting that he had been a cabin steward on a number of Caribbean cruise ships, a union card, and a forged Canadian passport which gave his name as Don Temple of Timmons, Ontario.

At nine the next morning he was interviewed by the captain of the ship, a middle-aged Australian named Chris Watkins.

"If Rocque sent you," he growled, "then that means you're some kind of criminal. It also means that you're all right and you won't try any shit on my boat, will you now, Don?"

"Just looking for a job, Captain. I don't want any trouble."

"You ever done one of these private charters?"

"No, Captain."

"They're a bitch. They don't bother me or the crew much, these damn rich people, but they make the cabin staff work like hell. They don't know a fucking thing about sailing, but they know plenty about how they like their martinis, so that's where they exert their authority. If they give you an order, you obey it."

"Just like a cruise, Captain."

"No it isn't," snapped Watkins. "You think like that and you'll be better off leaving this job be. You're not a cabin waiter on some floating brothel with three thousand dentists on board, you are the hired slave of the charterer. Got it?"

"Yes, Captain."

"Good. The ship is in berth eight in Monte. We sail at five on the evening tide—well, not really on the evening tide, but I'm supposed to say things like that on board. It makes the rich fuckers think they're being nautical." For the first time, Watkins grinned. "So I want you aboard at eleven. Henny—he's the chief steward, Filipino—he'll give you a uniform and instruct you in your duties."

"Fine, Captain."

"Aww shit, you only have to call me captain when the charterers are aboard. Rest of the time, call me Chris."

"Fine, Chris."

"There's just one more rule, Don. And this is the big one for charter work . . ."

"Fire away."

"Don't talk to, look at, or even think about the women that come aboard. They're not for you."

"Got it."

Watkins shook hands. "Welcome aboard, Don." He grinned again. "Or whatever your name is."

* * *

Henny was a tiny, cheerful, wizened Filipino man who looked Paine up and down.

"You awful big for yacht work. You're gonna bump your head all the time."

They were standing on the deck of the *Sea Dawn*. The ship was vast, easily two hundred feet, probably more, and it didn't look to Paine as if there would be much of a space problem.

Henny seemed to read his thoughts. "Not up here. I mean down in crew's quarters, in the galley. They keep all the room for the passengers. We have to crawl into little spaces."

"I'll manage."

Henny gave him a uniform. White ducks, white shoes, white socks, a white shirt, and a white mess jacket with *Sea Dawn* embroidered on the left breast. Paine had never felt so ridiculous in his entire life.

"You look good," pronounced Henny. "Your uniform get dirty, change it. Immediately! Now I show you around."

The *Sea Dawn* was luxuriously fitted with nine huge cabins, a living room, two dining rooms, a pool room, and half a dozen other unnautical features like saunas and gyms.

"Steward only serve. You don't have to cook, but sometime you have to make drink. You know how to make drink?"

"Yeah," said Paine, "some drinks."

"What's a double bloody bull?"

"A what?"

241

Henny held his head and groaned. "I give you *Old Mr. Boston Bar Guide* tonight. You study it and hope tonight they just want white wine. The passengers come aboard at four."

"How many are there?"

"Four. Two couples."

That didn't sound like an impossible number to handle. Henny had already explained that there was a morning steward as well, two cooks, a laundryman, a pair of valets, and a chambermaid, as well as a crew of eight. All that to take care of four people.

"When am I on duty?"

Henny laughed and showed a lot of teeth. "Don, you always on duty."

The passengers arrived at dockside at the stroke of four. Two Rolls-Royces pulled up at the gangplank, and the chauffeurs nearly fell over themselves trying to open the doors fast enough. Watkins had called the entire crew to the taffrail, standing more or less at attention, to welcome the charterers aboard.

First up the plank was Norman Allison, a portly, gray-haired man whom Henny had informed him was a major producer in Hollywood. Henny, who read *Variety* faithfully to keep up on the names he was likely to serve, had been excited: "He produce *Deadly Intent*. You see that? Grossed one hundred and fifty million. He produced *Deadly Intent Two*. That grossed two hundred million domestic!"

Allison was accompanied by another man, his

attorney, Stephen Brademan, another figure well-known to Henny. "He represent all the big stars." Henny reeled off half a dozen names that meant nothing to Paine. He hardly ever went to the movies.

Both men were with women in their twenties, both of almost stupefying beauty. One, a tall, leggy blonde with wide-set blue eyes and full red lips, was introduced as Mrs. Allison. The other, a dark French girl with smoky brown eyes and a perpetual pout, was Miss Boulanger. She was with Brademan.

Watkins took them over the ship, then the two valets whisked them to their staterooms. The crew, mostly French or Corsican, took their positions—Watkins wasn't going out under sail, but he knew the importance of putting on a good show—muttering among themselves about the beauty of at least two of the passengers.

As the *Sea Dawn* nosed out beyond the break-water and into the Mediterranean, a lone man stood on the terrace of the famous aquarium that fronted the bluff of Monte Carlo. He followed the vessel out to sea through high-powered binoculars, catching a glimpse of John Paine working his way aft along the starboard railing of the ship. The man cursed aloud.

"Where are you going, Paine?" he whispered under his breath. There were few people at the aquarium, which was about to close. And no one was close enough to recognize that the words had been spoken in Russian.

Norman Allison leaned against the rail of the open deck to the rear of the main salon watching the skyline of Monte Carlo recede behind him. He had been advised to take the cruise for his health, but he didn't want to. He had three films in preproduction in Hollywood, and another that was about to start shooting in New York. Being out on a boat in the middle of the Mediterranean was not his idea of a good time. He had also been advised to swear off hard liquor. But the hell with that. If he was supposed to relax, then he would do it his way.

He caught sight of Paine. Allison hadn't listened to the names of the crew members. Why should he even bother himself with them? They all worked for him anyway. He turned to Paine.

"Boy. Get me a gin and tonic."

"Yes, sir," said John Paine.

SPECIAL PREVIEW

*Here are the opening scenes
from*

ROGUE AGENT #2
Hard to Kill

On sale now!

"Tits like this," said Hugo. He held his hands out in front of his chest, palms upward and open as if weighing handfuls full of air.

"*Op la*," Mike said, and writhed in his bunk. "You seen them?"

"Sure," said Hugo. "Like this." He closed his hands, grabbing air.

"You not to talk about the women," said Henny unhappily. "That causes trouble. Only trouble."

"Shut up, chink," snapped Hugo.

"I'm not chink," said Henny indignantly. "I'm from Philippines."

"Same fuckin' thing," said Hugo, illustrating his contempt with a long, sonorous fart.

"*Op la*," said Mike.

"Hey, Don," yelled Hugo, although Don was only a bunk away, "why don't you go get some beer?"

Don Temple didn't look up from the book he

was reading. "Fuck you. Get it yourself."

"You're the steward; you get it. It's your job."

"Not to get beer for shitheads like you, you skaggy motherfucking prick."

"*Op la*," said Mike. Henny laughed.

"Fuckin' deck steward talking to me like that." Hugo hauled himself up in his bunk. "You bastard, I'm gonna punch your teeth in."

Don Temple, the Canadian deck steward on the luxury oceangoing yacht *Sea Dawn*, glanced contemptuously at Hugo, one of the deckhands. "Are you always so fucking noisy?"

Hugo hopped off his bunk and swaggered toward Temple. "Now I'm gonna fix your face for you, you fuckin' bastard."

Temple put down his book, part of the giant library of pornography that could be found in the cramped crew's quarters. It was a tattered, stained paperback called *The Cunning Linguist*.

"Hugo," he said, pointing at some of the heating pipes that snaked across the gray steel ceiling. "You see that?"

"What?"

"*That*." Temple was pointing at a brass handle of a heating duct, a faucet that could be opened or closed to adjust the heating in the room.

Hugo jammed his thumbs into the pockets of his white pants. "Yeah, I see that, you fuckin' Canadian bastard. What about it, you bastard?"

"If you give me any trouble, I will make you eat that," said Temple over his shoulder.

"You'll *what?*"

"I'll make you eat it."

Henny, the Filipino chief steward, looked worried. "Hey, boys, I think this go far enough." Hugo was a big bruiser and a veteran of a thousand bar fights in a hundred ports of call around the world. Henny had seen him fight before, and he fought dirty. Temple was a big man too, but quiet, and a waiter; there was nothing in his background that said that he could take a man like Hugo, in a fair fight or foul. Henny had a feeling that Temple was just talking big, hoping that the big Frenchman would back down.

"Oh yeah? We'll see about that." Hugo took another menacing step toward Temple's bunk.

"Please, boys ..." pleaded Henny. "Mike, tell them to stop."

Mike was lying on his bunk, grinning. He was a wiry little Englishman, the laundryman on the *Sea Dawn*. He had spent most of his life in France and spoke the language like a native. He was also—as he freely admitted—a dyed-in-the-wool coward. "Sorry, Henny, I'm not going to get mixed up in this. These lads are a bit big for me to handle."

Henny gulped. If Temple got hurt, he couldn't do his duties. The rich people who had chartered the *Sea Dawn* didn't like having deck stewards show up for work with stitches on their faces, black eyes, or big, scabby cuts.

"Aww, come on, please, boys."

"Yeah, please, boy," said Temple, going back to his book.

Hugo smiled. Temple was a coward and was backing down. That meant he had him. There was nothing Hugo liked more than beating up some weak bastard who talked tough but had nothing to back it up with. He leaned in.

"Chicken."

"You're in my light," said Temple.

"'You're in my light,'" mimicked Hugo in a faggy falsetto. He worked his jaws a moment and them squirted a stream of warm spittle onto the pages of *The Cunning Linguist.* In return he received Temple's sharp elbow straight and unerring in his throat.

"Ack." The big man choked and staggered back, holding his bruised windpipe.

"Boys!" shrieked Henny.

Temple whipped off his bunk and neatly put Hugo's huge head in a hammerlock. Then, as if lifting a ballerina, he shot him straight up into the tangle of heating pipes on the low ceiling. There was a dull bong as Hugo's head connected with metal. Swiftly Temple dragged Hugo forward a few feet until they stood under the brass handle. He grabbed a handful of Hugo's black, sweaty hair and yanked, pulling his head back. "See it?" hissed Temple. "See it, you Frog bastard?"

Temple bent his knees, a plié, and then vaulted the big sailor up to the faucet, jamming his face against it. "Take a nice big bite."

"Fuck you!"

Temple applied more pressure, forcing Hugo's face into the unyielding metal, his lips tearing on the brass. "Take a big bite, Hugo."

Hugo growled and opened his mouth and bit down on the brass ring with his big yellow teeth.

"Harder."

Hugo ground his teeth against the metal.

"Good?"

Hugo managed to spit out some incoherent obscenities.

"I said, is it good?" Temple jammed his face against the metal a little harder. "Tell me it's good."

"Tell him!" yelled Henny. "He kill you."

"It's good," growled Hugo.

Temple let him fall to the deck in a heap and placed his foot on Hugo's neck like a hunter posing with a trophy. "Listen to me," he said quietly. "Don't ever fuck with me again. Do you understand?"

Hugo nodded.

Temple released him. "Good."

Hugo rolled away and stood up, glaring at Temple. "One day I'll kill you."

Temple shook his head. "No you won't." Every man in the cabin believed him.

Hugo glared at Mike, who was smirking at him. Mike liked trouble, as long as he wasn't involved personally. "What are you looking at, asshole?"

Mike looked away. "Nothing, *mon vieux*."

Hugo rolled into his bunk and turned his face to the wall. Being beaten in a fight was bad enough; being beaten and humiliated by a steward was unbearable. He touched his torn lips and swore silently he would get even.

A bell rang. Henny, relieved that the whole thing was over, looked at the board, which told the crew which passenger was summoning which servant. "Deck steward" had lit up, along with "main salon."

"That you, Don. Make sure you don't have blood on your uniform."

Temple slipped into his mess jacket, a short white bolero with the words "Sea Dawn" embroidered on the breast. Henny straightened his bow tie and then pushed him toward the gangway. "Remember polish the tray before you get there."

"Yes, Henny." Don Temple climbed up from the cramped crew's quarters to the palatial upper reaches of the ship.

There was silence after he left, but the three men in the cabin were all wondering the same thing: where had Temple learned to fight like that?